I AM NOT YOUR EVE

I AM NOT
YOUR EVE

Devika Ponnambalam

Bluemoose

First published in 2022 by
Bluemoose Books Ltd
25 Sackville Street
Hebden Bridge
West Yorkshire
HX7 7DJ

www.bluemoosebooks.com

British Library Cataloguing-in-Publication data
A catalogue record for this book is available from the British Library

Hardback 978-1-910422-89-2

Softback 978-1-915693-05-1

Printed and bound in the UK by Short Run Press

For Appa

She lives, whom we call dead.

Henry Wadsworth Longfellow,
from the poem *'Resignation'.*

Eight days have gone since I followed you from there to here.

The *tiare* blossom you plucked, and brought me this morning, gives out a scent so fierce, it hides the sweat of you, which clings to this pillow, my *pareu*, the shadows.

I pretend I'm curled up beneath the ocean, or the bed of a river, in a hollow, while the dogs bark on dry land, their cries muffled by the strong wall of water, above, all around me.

The women still pray to Hina – do you hear? They go, behind one another, in secret, in the white man's cloth, to the old worshipping places. The men have also gone away. They've climbed into the mountains, and their dugout canoes. And every hut stands empty, from Tahiti Iti to Tahiti Nui, and back again. The trees outside, beyond, at the edge, on the banks, are ripe with flower, each one like us, dreaming of a time, opening to the sun.

You come to me, and whisper, I have a present for you. You show me your closed fist. It makes me flinch. But. In the palm of your hand, lies a pair of copper earrings.

You wanted these, remember?

You remembered. They glint, your gift, in the half-light of this half-life, for me, your half-wife.

The river gurgles.
   The sea yawns.
   The lizard scuttles.
   The leaves whisper.
   The ground rustles.
   The mountains are silent though.
   The bamboo creaks.
   The dog sings.
   And the cockerel whines.

They tell me, when I was born, I screamed so loud, my cry carried all the way to Taravao, and the hawkers ceased their calling, and just for a few moments, the market place was completely still.

They tell me, when I was born, I would only find peace in the sound of the flame, crackling. Did I imagine a ghost beyond these walls? Or a footstep on a fallen leaf; invisible like the cicadas on the branches of the trees?

When I was four, or five, or six, I imagined a boat without an outrigger cutting through dark water, travelling towards our shores, guided by the summit of Mount Orohena. I heard it groaning with the weight of all that wood, its big heavy body, bringing with it more white men. And my heart beat, a distant drum, a familiar hum, in the shadows of our one-room hut.

And I listened to my Foster Mother's breath, her long sighs and low whistle, and I eased myself from her flesh, and it was easy.

And I crawled like a dog, when I was four, or five, or six, all the way to the edge of the opening, where the oil lamp still burned, now silent and steady. And I spoke the words I knew nothing of:

You will not die, for God knows when you eat of it your eyes will be opened, and you will be like God, just like Him, knowing good, from evil.

And I listened carefully, to the quietness. For a step, a breath, for Hina beating her *tapa* on the moon.

3

Dear Diary,

Today, news finally arrived. Maman refused to speak a word of it, and instead, took herself to the far end of the dining table, away from our prying eyes. She read Papa's letter not once, but twice, then a third time – until I am sure she had digested every ounce of information contained within. I, meanwhile, flitted about the room like a bird waiting for a scrap, and after an insufferable half hour, she folded the piece of paper in two and pushed it beneath the palm of her hand.

She sat there calmly, caressing her gold wedding band, looking out over the dark rooftops beyond, her thoughts a complete mystery to me. All she would say was – when it rains in Copenhagen, it feels like it will never end. I made the bold decision to go to her then and placed my head upon her shoulder, so wild was I to know the contents of that letter. But she shrugged me off as one discards a wet mantle. Maman, I pleaded, unable to contain myself. Crocodile tears, she replied, watching me cry, coolly, green shadows beneath her gray eyes.

Finally, relenting, she pushed the folded letter towards me. C had already taken his leave, and P, throwing me a look that said, "I could not care less", sloped off as well. How wonderful it was to feast my eyes on my darling's writing hand! Even the smell of him seemed to emanate from that musty sheet of paper. Papa says he is sorely disappointed and should have known better. We, meaning The French, have plundered Paradise like bold devils, and killed off The Noble Savage, whilst the natives wear clothes inflicted upon them by The Missionaries. In the main port town, they live in houses with roofs of galvanized tin, and are proud of this, though the women, he says, still carry an innate sense of grace, a certain *noa noa*. Papa likens it to the scent of the earth mixed with the purity of the *tiare* blossom, which grows in profusion all year round. He tells Maman she would also approve of the native men who are tall and lean,

4

because she has a taste for things of beauty – a generous remark to a woman who does not have one good word for her husband!

Papa has decided to live further inland, away from the authorities, and has bargained for himself a traditional hut with bamboo walls and a leaf roof. He will live in quiet contemplation, and make countless studies, in order to begin the important work he has gone there to do. He requires a little help to keep him afloat because he does not possess the strength to climb the mountains for the abundant fruit, or the required skills to catch the fish that live in the lagoons. He feels quite useless in that respect and must rely on food from the general store, which is expensive because it has to be imported. He has not heard from Monfreid and promises that as soon as he is settled, he will send word for all of us to join him. When I repeated this last line out loud, Maman snorted. She said that he was deluded and she would be too if she were to wrench us away from this secure existence to live in a hut on some distant, and precarious shore. It sounded wonderful to me. At least we would be relieved of this incessant rain, would we not? Maman did not reply. Was she thinking of that place, where the warm waves lapped? We heard the front door opening then. It was Mormor back from her errands. Maman snatched up the letter, almost tearing it in the act, and pressed a finger to her lips. She tucked Papa's letter away in the bodice of her dress, deep between her bosoms.

Tonight, the world wears a black shroud. The rain has not abated but developed into a fine mist, falling silently, and the moment Papa bid us farewell comes to mind. Maman had informed him that morning (I am sure), I was a lady now.

How pensive he looked as he spoke those last words to me. Thirteen, and you are a lady now.

Once, a long time ago, the men launched their dugouts from the black sand, navigated their way across the lagoon, through the reef pass, towards a boat without an outrigger. They did not hear the waves, or the drums being struck, just their hearts, while the ancient priest's words stood, powerful as the mountains behind them. On the deck of that great vessel, they glimpsed the men who would tear them in two, who possessed skin the colour of day, and eyes, clear as morning sky.

They were the white gods that would come from across the circle of the sea, and they had arrived; they were now here.

Once, on a piece of land jutting out into the bay, a *marae* was built from limestone and coral rock, in honour of a god who'd loved a mortal girl, and she gave birth to all of Tahiti, her name was Vairaumati. The priests sent the women and children, the dogs and the cockerels into the valley during this building time, which was *tapu*.

The birds beat their wings in the trees nearby and boldly sang, the only sound allowed.

Once, long ago, the bones of a defeated clan were placed on that *marae*. Man, woman, and child were laid out in rows, three feet deep, on the altar, or strung up between the branches of the *miro* trees. They became a garland of skulls, the unfortunate ones, bordering that sacred place, a twisted cord passed through each ear canal.

Once, there was a temple to a god whose names are uttered now only by the driving rain. Today, another temple stands over what once was, with thick white walls, cool to the touch. It possesses a door cut from a tree, which belonged to the first generation of roots on this land. A door that leads to the God our Father and the God his Son, who hangs with arms outstretched, his ribs showing through pale, wondrous skin.

When the rains come, sometimes without warning, bowl upon bowl, they fill every lake and cold-water pool to the brim.

The mountains are not quiet then. The water pours from the crests of the valley, not in a trickle, but with a roar, thundering down to the rivers below, out into the lagoon, and the mouth of the open seas.

In the shelter of the mango trees, the white terns coo, they take rest, they cower from the flooding rains, which carry on falling, never ending. And I wait, like the cockerel waits, patiently, listening to the drumbeat on your *pandanu* leaf roof. Between the shadows of your roof, shielded from the wild-pouring rain, the long-winding rain, I watch the lizard as he creeps along, upside down, now still as a statue, a leaf, his eyes wide open in the sticky heat. The lizard, he tells me:

When the rains come, they will fall, with all their strength, without a moment's breath. The rivers will break their banks, and the water will destroy the taro fields, the sweet potato, and the wild, wild yam. When it enters inside, when it reaches the foot of your bed, do not be afraid. Leave your lover, and go quietly, and take down his adze...do you hear?

I open my eyes. You lie beside me like a dead man, your pillow scrunched up beneath your neck, legs and arms splayed. The rain sounds like many things, my heart beating, your heart beating, your heart beats, the rain falls. I listen to it in the dense dark. It does not stop.

Your adze hangs from its hook on the wall, beside the doorway, in the same place, always.

Dear Diary,

The last time I saw Papa, he spoke of the promise I made when I was five; that I would be his wife when I grew up. I told him I did not remember it, so ashamed was I. The words lay upon my chest, like pebbles, too heavy to shake off. But I do remember, as if it were yesterday.

It was one summer evening, and we were still living in Rue Carcel. I had gone down to the end of the garden to the glass house, where once there had been plants, but which now contained Papa's studio, "because of the light". Maman had relented, unwillingly. She reminded him she had chosen this home precisely because of the garden and its glass house.

Papa was rinsing out his brushes and cleaning his paint-stained hands with a rag soaked in turpentine, when I took it from him and finished off the task, rubbing the dried colour from between his fingernails. He had used a lot of blue that day which had now turned black. When I looked up at him, he was smiling, eyes glimmering, wet with tears, and it was then. Then, that I gave him my promise.

The last time I saw Papa, his appearance caused quite a stir in the house. He was wearing the same embroidered waistcoat and his hair had grown so long it skimmed the tops of his shoulders. When he first laid eyes upon me here in the hallway, he shook his head, and asked three times, is it really you? Then, finally accepting my answer, he replied, how big you've grown, and the image of your Grandmother!

These words did not fill Maman with joy and she demanded he follow her into the living room where his sons were waiting, though he would not let go of my hand all evening. I felt bad for my brothers, but I was secretly happy, delirious to be exact.

Papa has promised to write me a diary whilst he is in Tahiti. He will fill it with his thoughts and observations, and when I join him, it will be like I had been there all along. Sometimes, I imagine he is still here, holding me, speaking in the way that he does, with the utmost tenderness. He tells me not to fight with C and to be good for Maman, to take care of one another, and to keep our love sacred.

Papa did not share Maman's bed that night. After dinner, where hardly a word was spoken between the two, he rose, putting his fedora back on his head and declared – I must be going before they are fully booked at the inn. Maman would not answer when I asked her why. She simply said, with eyes fixed firmly on her empty plate, the gravy sullied with steak blood – yes, go now and get ahead of the queue. Then Papa left without another word, giving my fingers one last squeeze. He planted a kiss on C's head and held out his hand to P, who refused to take it. How my heart ached for him at that moment, and how it raged against my elder brother!

These days, Maman is always in the blackest of moods. Yesterday, she told me I am just like my father. Of that, I am glad. If I dare challenge her, she will give me the silent treatment for days upon end, and I know she goes snooping about in my room (just as I do in hers), looking for letters, and clues to my disobedience. I have therefore taken to hiding my diary at the bottom of my trunk, beneath my old dolls. I will throw it in the fire when I die, and no one will ever know what I feel, what I once felt, in my heart of hearts.

I have penned a poem for Papa, but I wonder. Will he ever see it?

How about this?

Tehura, my fifteen-year old *vahine*, is lying on my bed in the dark...I know you're not fifteen but let's say you are, so they don't crucify me upon my return – if I can make the pool in the grotto bigger than it really is, the colour of ripe cherries, I can make you fifteen. Now, where were we? Ah, yes, lying on my bed in the dark...

Tehura, my fifteen-year old *vahine*, is lying on my bed in the dark, the lamp unlit, the oil run out, and I have still not returned from Papeete, as I had promised I would. The coach has broken down, but she is not to know that, my Tehura, and imagines me drinking and dancing with the whores in the town's one bar. In truth, I'm making the long journey home by foot, the moon my guide in the great night sky.

It is almost two in the morning when I finally reach Mataiea, and Tehura, hearing my footsteps approach, is now frozen with fear. She thinks me the *tupapau* come to eat her up, no flame in her lamp to keep them out. Transfixed on our bed, she glimpses a shape at the door, my shadow in the half-darkness. And only when I speak her name does she realise it is I. She sobs with relief as I kneel down beside her, and scolds me like a mother her child, and makes me promise to never leave her again so alone without any light.

What do you think, my darling, of the story of the painting?

You do not wait for my thoughts. Instead, you get down on your hands and knees and crawl towards me, your eyes the colour of a breadfruit leaf, yellowing. You pick up the *tiare* blossom from where it fell, and try to place it behind my ear. But I push your hand away, and tell you, I don't want a dead flower.

A dog barks, the sea churns, the church bell rings.

My dress lies crumpled in the middle of your dirt floor, where I dropped it. Your stool is littered with scraps of your stale French bread. It is what I swallow morning and evening, along with meat from the tins. This new life is not what I imagined. I thought it would be better than marrying a fisherman, because he would only bring me fish to eat everyday. But how I long for it, now, for that one luxury.

I imagine your stool holds upon it a large piece of raw *tunny*, a green papaya, two mangos, red-edged, and the scent of wild bananas, ripening.

I want to get up, pull my dress over me, but I know not to, I know I must have your permission first. So I curl, naked as I am, to the shape of a boulder, my forehead kissing to my knees, as I would have, once, long ago, when I was safe, not knowing anything. My Foster Mother would roll my fingers between her own, praying for them to be long and tapered, for them to be beautiful. And she smoothed my nose each day with her fingertips so it would sit wide and flat on my dark face. She bit my eyelashes to stubs so they would grow thick like grass, and she whispered the names of the gods and the men whose stories live on the tongue and in the shadows.

You bring me a perfect white *tiare* blossom, its fragrance sharp and sweet, and you tuck it behind my ear, very gently.

Before that moment, those moments of intimacy and greed, a seed took root in Birth Mother's belly. And for ten full moons, a girl with her own unique identity unfurled slowly in the silence of that world. Fed and watered by the grace of her creator.

She was just an egg-shaped thing, a pendant on a string, turning in an ocean of dark, without thought, or mind or reason, a light below the surface. Gently flickering.

For two hundred and seventy-one days, her body grew, but not her experience. This was her first journey.

At the end of her eighth month, she could smile. She frowned, fanned her fingers and toes, opened and closed her eyes, her perfectly formed mouth. She even covered ears at offending noises. Her heart, which had taken shape first, now beat with impatience. She yearned to be free of her cramped surroundings. Her hands, the size of two swollen plums, made fists, but there was nothing to hold, just yet. Her blood flowed from the right of the base of the great foundation and from the left her mother's blood flowed.

The world was being made. And he was not alone in his making, Ta'aroa. He had a helper. One who'd fashioned the mountains from his backbone, the strong earth from his thighs. Yes, Ta'aroa had a helper.

At the end of her ninth month, she turned, twisting the right way, instinctively, with determination. Her legs and arms were not buds anymore, and her spine ached to unfold itself. She craned her neck, eyes closed, facing the opening.

Birth Mother's countenance, usually calm, always serene, now distorted with agony, her cry joining the chorus of a hundred cicadas outside her door, which was not solid, but an open portal to the mountains beyond. The moon hung in the lamp-black night, the shape of a claw.

Birth Mother cried out to let her child know she was there, within the bamboo reed walls, and waiting. She wanted to scream too, the girl, but could not, her voice stifled by water, and yet, her mind was bursting with a desire to be free. This was her first emotion.

That push, that escape out from the dark into light was her second journey, and it was fraught with danger. But the stars, each one, were gathered together, hands joined in perfect alignment.

She moved through a corridor of heat, flesh, and blood, with her placenta following closely behind. The sacred cord, cut swiftly by the Foster Mother, was wrapped in scented cloth, and would be buried deep in the mountain in the shade of a *tamanu* tree, with a prayer to keep the child's living spirit safe.

She took a breath, her first.

Then released her voice through a set of tiny but powerful lungs. She was in the real world now and she trembled with rage, with the shock of it; her fateful decision to leave the glittering hut of dreams where she had breathed water like an eel to become a girl who would tread paths, rocks, and black sand.

A girl who would breathe air and open her eyes to the light.

When 'Iripa'u caught Huahine, he threw her down on her back, and her legs, the spreading of her legs, became both sides of the bay. When 'Iripa'u pushed himself, his penis into her vagina, her sex became the body of that land, the island, which today carries her name.

When Huahine cried out during this act of violation, 'Iripa'u's men coolly watched, then they also took their turns, clasping her wrists and ankles to the earth. When Huahine's voice ricocheted across the valleys, her elder brother flew to her, but on finding her, chose to keep himself hidden, trembling like a leaf on a midnight breeze.

He watched as his sister fastened her mouth around 'Iripa'u's penis, saw her spit him out, so that he became a mountainous peak. And the crest of 'Iripa'u can be seen to this day by travellers, far out at sea.

When she died, Huahine, of grief, her sex, the shape of a flower, a tiare blossom grew, replacing her entirely. They say her beauty lies in her sex, not her face, because it is the flower that carries her features, her brow, her cheekbones, her eyes, and her scent pervades to this day, over the high plateaus, and the low-lying emerald groves.

When 'Iripa'u stumbled away, clutching his wound, his other hand reached out to brush the water, and from this gesture, his body also became an island, which is now called Taha'a, and he lies beside her, the flower of the woman, in the ocean, this man.

I fell into a bottomless pit again today,
Stumbled into it.
Didn't see it coming.
My eyes fill with chandelier teardrops,
As I think of you.

The daughter leaves her mother's womb from that same mythic opening, the first doorway, out into a room with four solid walls, five oil lamps burning, and six unlit candles on a high chandelier, cloaked in a thick layer of dust.

The daughter is delivered by an old family physician, who cannot tell if she is a girl or a boy, his spectacles misplaced in the melee. It is the maid that confirms the sex, and proceeds to take charge, entrusted by the lady of the house. She sponges the quiet baby clean, and despite nerves of steel, her hands tremble with the importance of the task. The daughter is placed into the arms of her mother, who smiles at the new addition, a delicate thing, and gives a kiss to its soft, sweet brow. The child succumbs, keeping her eyes half closed, so they appear the colour of dark berries. The mother nods towards the closed door and returns her baby to the maid, who takes it wordlessly, and slips out of the room.

The daughter is then presented to The Painter, who has been pacing the hallway, forever it would seem, waiting discreetly, as all nineteenth century gentlemen must. And the first words he whispers to his girl-child are – you are a savage like me, your father – and she responds with a cry that resounds throughout the house, every room.

The Painter gazes at his creation, with pride, and a joy overflowing as she opens her eyes wide. They are big and light, brown, almost gold, and he falls in love with her, his next muse, his first daughter, after a long line of boys. At that moment, without hesitation, or even consultation, he decides to name her after his own mother, the woman who died when he was five, and by dying, became his lost queen. His half-Indian mother, his Inca-blooded mother who belongs to the garden of his soul, the first garden, his first true Eve.

You tell me not to move while you make me. You tell me to cross my ankles, to lie like that, to keep on looking at you. You ask me what I am thinking. You snort like a pig when I reply, nothing.

Nothing? Yes, it's better that way.

I'll put some thoughts in your head, you say, create a story around this picture to rival Manet's Olympia, a story to whet their appetites, the critics, the pathetic monkeys who don't know their heads from their tails.

She has been brought here, without her consent, and pinned above the doorway of The Painter's hut, a world so far removed from all she once knew. It is, however, a marked improvement from the darkness she inhabited, trapped for three whole months between the pages of a sketchbook, with only the sounds of a creaking ship and lapping waves for company.

She is resigned to her fate. To sharing her days with the creature in the roof, which tries at every opportunity, she is sure, to unnerve her. It watches from the shadows where the light does not fall, has lodged itself deep, between the leaves, neatly camouflaged. It watches with eyes of yellow amber, and possesses a tongue so quick it would cover the entire length of her body, if it wished. She knows this and trembles at the idea.

She has travelled to the other side of the world, across five oceans and three continents, for just one reason.

To provide him with the inspiration he needs in order to create a masterpiece of his own.

He was merely one in a long line of them, the post-impressionists, as they liked to be called, the pretentious, joyless, slimy know-it-alls, the poets, and philosophers, the cretins, they all came, joined hands with the painters under the veil of debate.

I got passed around like a bottle of vintage Beaujolais. I'm not bitter; it was my choice.

Where you see me now, in this *carte postale*, a lovely reproduction of the original I might add, I am at the height of my powers, my prowess, just beginning. I was just nineteen when dear Edouard plucked me off the streets, one November afternoon, the sky the colour of bone. He made me his Olympia. Took me to all the soirees, the ones to be seen at, at least. Paraded me around like a precious poodle, his wife, daughter, bourgeois whore. He introduced me to his eager followers, his peers, with my clothes on of course, though they knew every inch of me, or imagined they did.

They fell at my feet, and parted with their meagre incomes and inheritances as one does one's bodily functions, these scroungers of long-suffering wives. They gave everything they had for me to spread my legs, on a table, a chaise lounge, but never a bed. And I submitted without a moment's regret, happily bled them dry with relish. He was no different, the one that lies, that rises, that wipes his juices clean on the blue and yellow printed cloth, which her mother has wrapped the wretched Bible in. He places his breath upon her neck and insists he is not like other men. He told this to me too, once, dear god, why are they all the same? It was his mantra:

I am different to other men. I will leave this cesspit, this hellhole they think is the centre of the world, and I will find my Eden.

Can you sit still for a long time without moving? Will you come, and live with me, forever? Are you scared?

I said yes to forever. I did not know what sitting still for a long time meant, but I said yes, and to the last question, I said no. Even though, I am. I was. Scared.

They watch as I draw near, fingertips brushing my arms, my shoulders, my hips, my thighs, they tell me, go inside and meet your man! They watch, as I sit down on the soles of my upturned feet, watch as you ask your questions and I answer.

When I dare to look up, to really look, I see eyes, not blue, not green, but somewhere in between, eyes careful and cautious, and deep as holes, a hooked nose, a chin, long and square. You are not so old, but not very handsome, your teeth stained yellow, but I hope you will be kind, because you are a white man. And because of that, they tell me I am lucky.

Foster Mother places the Good Book in the middle of her *pareu*, which clothed me on the day of my birth, drops a ripe mango on top, then gathers up its edges. She makes for me a leaving parcel, tying the knot tight, and gives me the oil lamp, not asking if you also have one. Remember, she says, light it each night, and place it just inside the opening.

And I imagine you possess a door. It is heavy, and when it shuts, makes a noise like thunder.

Birth Mother pushes past the wall of people, takes your arm boldly, and says – she must come back in eight days if she is not happy. The smile on your face disappears, and a deep crease forms between your eyes, which are not the colour of the sea any more but the sky, darkening. You turn to my Foster Mother and ask, who is this woman? She is the Birth Mother, and I am the Foster Mother, she replies.

This woman grew her in her body in the land of *po*, but I fed her afterwards with my milk in the land of *ao*. You see, here in Tahiti, we have more than one mother. I also had two.

Once, a long time ago, the men launched their dugouts from the black sand, navigated their way across the lagoon, through the reef pass, towards a boat without an outrigger.

Once, not long ago, she tumbled out of Birth Mother's womb into a room thick with shadows, its walls made of bamboo reed, which creaked and were buffeted by the wind. Like a hundred doors opening, and closing. There was just one oil lamp burning, and she rolled in a dress of bright blood onto a mat woven with the leaf of *pandanus*.

They cleaned her, Foster Mother and Taneipa with river-water collected in wooden gourds at dawn. The sun had been a burning disc then rising up from the depths of the sea, turning the water all the colours of her birth.

She screamed again and again, releasing long held cries from deep within her diminutive body. She opened pearl-black eyes, blinking into the violet shadows, and the first person she saw was Taneipa, who matched her gaze with the same pair of eyes. She pushed a fist into the open palm of her sister's hand while Foster Mother clung to her, secretly thanking the old gods for this blessing.

They wrapped her in a midnight blue *pareu* etched with flowers, the stalks, and petals stained a brilliant yellow. The cloth that would follow her from this hut to the next, then on to her death.

Drunk on *kava*, The Father stumbled inside, tripping over his own two feet, and almost falling flat on his face, but was saved the humiliation by Foster Mother's lightning hand. He managed to stay upright just long enough to christen his child, yet another girl. He gave her a name that would disappear as soon as the sun fell, a name with two meanings: a pool of water, or a rock pool at the mouth of a river that flows out towards the sea.

Taneipa watched her new sister with sorrowful eyes, but she did not cry. She teased open a fist now the size of a mango stone, and stroked the inside of her hand. It was soft and smooth, a virgin page. Then, with a prompt from Birth Mother, she reluctantly gave up her sweet doll, to the woman who would take her and make her, her own. She was just five years old Taneipa, and had never witnessed a birth before.

Before that moment, she believed all babies appeared, wrapped in cloth, beside the doorway, delivered by some unknown force, without a trace of blood on them. On the cusp of a clear blue day, Taneipa woke silently from her childhood dream. And Birth Mother, with a fear as narrow as the gaps between her bamboo reed walls, whispered seven precious words.

Then closed her eyes, without even touching this third offering that had come out of her.

She is yours, love and be happy.

Dear Diary,

Papa has run out of money and wants to know why he has not heard from Maman or Vollard, or Monfreid for that matter. If I write, I wonder, will it reach him? He marks the back of his envelopes, Papeete, Tahiti.

Mormor has come to learn of his letters, and yesterday, I heard her in the drawing room, scolding Maman. She was saying what a useless man Papa was. How he has sacrificed everything at the altar of his ideals. How morose he always was. He could not even hold down a simple job, one she'd gone to great lengths to arrange. And he took to hiding himself in the attic. She brought up the subject of Suzanne Sewing again, the cook, naked on their bed. How he had the audacity to request it be hung up in the hallway. Maman was silent all the while. Then Mormor's voice became softer. Nothing will come of tears, she said, we must be strong and united in the face of such adversity. You must ignore his pleas for help, let him run out of money and find his way home. And we shall not have him back until he smartens up his act and behaves like a true and proper husband, and father to his five children.

Papa was always true and proper. Yes, he did take to the attic for days upon end, sitting at his easel, studying his reflection in the mirror, eyes full of melancholy. In winter, he wore an overcoat in the house, and when I paid him a visit, he would proclaim, it's Arctic up here. Beware! At suppertime, the atmosphere was always tense at the table, the silence thick with portent. Once, Mormor deigned to ask, what have you been doing today? He replied, working.

Working, she prodded, at what?

I've done a self-portrait I am very happy with.

Are you going to get good money for this work?

I do not know, but I am becoming a better painter.

This food here on this table did not magically appear; your wife has been giving French lessons while you—

Maman stopped her short, grasping her own mother's arm. Then Papa slammed his hand down on the dining table making the silverware jump and rose, devouring a chicken leg as he went. He threw me a little wink at the door. I thought it funny but Maman not so. C carried on eating as if nothing had happened, and P looked at Papa's empty place with utter contempt.

I climbed the stairs today to the attic and sat on Papa's wooden chair, which he painted a deep forest green. I leaned into its high back and closed my eyes. It is as though his spirit remains. The easel has gone but the table where his paintbrushes once stood still stands, beneath the skylight, stained with flecks of red, white, black, and yellow. Papa looks sombre in his Self-Portrait in Front of the Easel. Half his face is in shadow. The weak winter light falls across the other half. I know my face belongs to his, but I do not recognise myself in that painting. He is handsome but already troubled, already lost to us. I want to speak with him. I'd ask him to turn towards me, to meet my eyes, and tell me about them – his hopes and wishes.

The painting has been left in the attic where Maman keeps things of no use. Perhaps it hurts her to look at him? Papa is gone, living his life, the one he has chosen, and we have all been left behind. I love Maman but I love Papa more.

He is my beating heart. He dwells within me, a burning flame that can never be extinguished.

When I was girl, I did not know the world, only tasting it in the grains of sand on my tongue. When I was a girl, I'd watch my Foster Mother lighting the lamp. She would do this as soon as the sun fell, like a coin into the gleaming bowl of the sea.

One day she told me to rise up from my place on her mat. She said, you must learn Teha'amana, learn how to make fire by friction, with *toa* wood and stone, we are not rich enough to possess matches.

Later, as I did just this, now with ease, watching the flame grow tall, I told her, The Missionary said it is nonsense, only the Lord's Prayer can protect us from ourselves. She did not reply, so I continued, what does that mean, "from ourselves"? She had been there when he'd said it, right beside me, the heat of her arm through the cloth of her dress mingling with mine. After a short time, she spoke.

Here is The Good Book in this hand of mine clasped, and there is the lamp, in the same place as always, burning. At night, our ancestors walk the land. They crawl out from their boxes where we hid them, in the caves high up. They slide down the mountainside, in between the trees, and wait just beyond these walls. Only a flame will hold them back, believe me.

I imagined the lamps then, burning, right across the island, from little Tahiti to big Tahiti, from its head to its tail, and I wondered if the spirits dared to enter the unlit room of the white man's temple, if they stood at the feet of the God our Son, or if Jehovah's words had the power to keep them out.

I picked up the baked *uru* and began pulling away at its charred exterior shell, while my Foster Mother opened The Good Book, and began to read, though I knew she could not, her eyes moving blindly over a language, ours, which The Missionary Henry Nott spent many years learning.

The soul is cast out blind when it leaves the body. It rises and flies out of the door, past the lighting of the lamps to the place of two stones. If it brushes the stone of death, it can never return. If it touches the stone of life, it must go on, to Mount Temehani where Tu-ta-horoa will tell it which road to take.

To the right lies the road to Pu-o-roo-i-te-ao where Roma-tane waits in Rohutu-noa-noa with maro 'ura, his red-feather girdle.

To the left, lies the road to the crater of Mount Temehani, the entrance to Pu-o-roo-i-te-po, where Ta'aroa resides with those who have taken the wrong path, kings and queens, fearless warriors, and fishermen, they all live here, according to his rule.

When their daily work is done, the punishing transportation of rocks from one bank to the next, Ta'aroa's prisoners sit, huddled together, in the darkness of Po, listening to the water dripping down the cold cave walls.

When his hunger must be sated, Ta'aroa's cooks pluck the waiting spirits indiscriminately and scrape them into a paste with the shell of a large clam, as a sweetening for his taro-root pudding.

But they do not die, the unlucky ones, they are resurrected, to work, to wait, to quake, and to become once again, food for the great god, Ta'aroa-nui-tuhi-mate, whose curse is death, deep in the crater of Mount Temehani.

I will wear a dress of pure white and it will not be the only one.

I will have a dress of every colour. And it will not matter that my skin is the shade of earth because you have chosen me, a man who makes human beings. It was not my choice. It was yours.

I said yes. Yes. Yes. No. Then followed you on your man-carrying pig, and now, there are two more horses waiting to carry us, all the way to Mataiea. Foster Mother stands before the crowd that has gathered, chest puffed out, proud as a frigatebird. She nods, her smile wide, giving me permission to go. Go, she says, silently, with another nod, but I want to ask, to remind her – I am returning in eight days, am I not?

Birth Mother stays half-hidden behind the whole village, which followed us here, her round, leaf-like eyes peering back at me, and I realise, for the first time, they are the shape of mine, exactly the same. I search for Taneipa's sweet face, she who laced her fingers through my own, who said, go and find out, when I asked, how does he make them, human beings?

May God guide you, guide you both and lead you to Eternal Day, said The Missionary, and bowed his head like a slow beast. Like the cows that bask at the foot of the mountainside, flapping their tails to keep the mosquitoes away. Then he took Sister's arm, and turned from us, and through the rosewood door, they went. That was before.

Blood drips from the garland of thorns they pushed into his head, from the iron they drove into his flesh, his own people.

I imagine he watches the women who crouch at his feet, piling the dead petals and stalks into the skirts of their dresses, which they gather up to reveal their strong dark legs. I imagine he watches them through the open window cutting down the flowers from flame trees, which shield the graveyard from the ocean breeze. He watches them fill the empty basket with fresh blossoms, petals like folded butterfly wings, dark pink, like knives, bright red.

And before they leave his house, the resting place of his wounded body, they will touch his toes, each woman, with their fingers, lightly, and they will ask for mercy. They will ask forgiveness for what they will do afterwards.

And they press the scent of him to their lips, which is of rosewood too. The women imagine he will reward them for their devotion, and he will reward us, their daughters, because we are his children, the children of God.

And they repeat his promise in all three tongues, the banished one, the first white man's, and yours, painter-man.

Te mau tamari a te atua.

We are the children of God.

Les enfants de Dieu.

Once, on a piece of land jutting out into the bay, a *marae* was built from limestone and coral rock, in honour of a god who'd loved a mortal girl, and she gave birth to all of Tahiti. Her name was Vairaumauti, she whispered, gazing into the river, the only mirror she'd ever known.

But the Vai'ha did not respond, it flowed soundlessly away, into lagoon, before merging with the powerful body of the sea. The sun had been balancing, as though from a string, teasing, taunting her, warming the black crown of her head, her eyelids, the swollen bud of her lips, her skin, every inch, penetrating the cheap cotton cloth of her missionary dress. She had been studying her face in the water, its pleasing proportions, when huge grey eels, brown-spotted and fearless, wove up from the riverbed.

Then Taneipa had arrived, out of breath, breaking the delicate skin of her contemplation. And now she was sitting beside the man who would make her, and they were all watching, the villagers, and the fishermen, The Gendarme's Wife who stood before the fence that separated the big house from the square. And the hawkers who'd heard her very first cry. They were silent once more, squatting behind their island's bounty, succulent fresh fruit, and flowers with a perfume strong enough to stir the dead. There were hats, and fans, and shells of all kinds, collected from waters, near and far.

At that moment, she felt like a prize *tunny* fish, dredged up from the ocean, and held aloft for all to see. They were looking at her, she was sure, with a strange and curious disgust. They were saying:

Who is she? What village does she come from? How did she manage to catch a white man? He does not dress like all the others. Does he keep his hair long? I've never seen a hat like that before. I wonder if he goes barefoot everywhere. He is a man who makes human beings with colour.

And this fact leaves the mouth of The Father, still intoxicated, but now by good quality rum, supplied by The Painter himself.

This fact travels onto the burnished brow of a young banana gatherer, across the earth-worn hands of an old jewelry seller who fashions earrings from copper and pendants from iridescent shells. Travels to the other side of the square, onto the jaded mouth of a sun-blackened fisherman.

This fact falls across the branches of the flame trees, now a whisper, between the crimson petals of its bloom, between the sharp yellow beak of the Mynah bird, and by the time it returns, to reach the Foster Mother, he is the man who made Pomare V on his deathbed, the last King of Tahiti, the man who had been invited into the palace by the grieving Queen herself. He is the man who has travelled here by the good grace of the King of France.

That is where she is going I suppose, to be made by him.

He must be important then, and rich.

Maybe he will take her back to France one day?

They all have real wives; they say they will, but they never do.

And the flower seller shakes her head, and the woman beside her nods in agreement, and they carry on squatting, the soles of their feet firmly rooted to the earth. At the tips of their toes, thick garlands of white *tiare* blossom lie heaped up, petals entwined with lime green fern leaves.

The ocean is spread out before them, all around, a mass of water with many mysteries beyond it, inside it, worlds they will never know.

The ocean undulates, a wall of moving flesh.

The blazing sun is a cool drink of water for me, a rock is nice, or the trunk of a tree. Except. There is always a threat, some danger lurking.

I prefer dark places. A roof. With its leaves tightly woven together. Where only a sliver of moonlight manages to poke through, or high up, in the eaves of a cave. But I'm here. Here I am, in the home of a white man, though he never cares to look. Just a tick, tick, ticking comes from the bottom of my well. His ancestors caused much trouble in this land. He knows this, and yearns for the time before.

I keep my tongue hidden, tightly curled inside me, like a human baby. I can whip it out faster than lightning when the need arises. Can use it to clean my outer eyelids with tender loving care. But it's my eyes, which are the things I am most proud of. Always closed, yet open to the world.

My ancestor had an island named after him. He was born from a woman who gave birth to an egg, then buried it in the sand. When it hatched, a boy emerged with the body of a lizard, or a lizard with the head of a boy, whichever way you like to look at it. She hid him, but he grew. And grew. If you make a promise, you must never break it, but we don't trust human beings, because they break them all the time.

My ancestor ran from his hiding place, crawled across the water and out along the reef pass. He jumped into the sea face down. The currents from the South, East and West took him, and he became an island.

I see him every day, the outline of his body, visible from Tahiti, the green and yellow jagged peaks of Mo'orea.

The white man lights his candle, and languishes alone. Human beings are lonely creatures, ultimately, very much like us. He eats stale bread and pretends it is steak. In his hands, he holds an imaginary knife and fork, and drinks from a bottle he hides only from himself. He stares into it, through it, and out of the doorway to a night dense with stars, and he pleads to the ghosts and the gods, which surround our hut. He says, I need to find myself a wife, a muse, a lover, an Eve, to make this garden real.

I prefer dark places.

She watches from her position above the doorway, where he has pinned her, the white woman, skin as creamy as coconut pulp, and a body, as beautiful as the moon. She lies there bolder than morning, one hand covering her sex. Her eyes meet mine with distaste and distrust, and she edges closer to the shadows within her room, towards the crack of the door that spills yellow light. I think she thinks I'm going to eat her up. She has a secret, but she will not tell it.

I try to bargain with her – if you tell me, I'll tell you the story of the lizard boy and why he ran from his mother who promised to feed him, take care of him, forever, until she died.

She uncovers her sex and conceals her mouth, the bracelet on her wrist flashing, a deep crease forming between the eyes, like a cut. I can hear her breath, hard and heavy. I listen to the world beyond her door, which seems very close, wheels turning on stone, and voices calling out to one another from near and far.

I wonder if I could live there, in that picture she inhabits. I could crawl, where she sprawls, and hide beneath her bed, for a while, couldn't I? She knows what I am thinking, I think, and looks at me, eyes now wide with wonder, revealing a sly smile. There's a flower growing there, a blooming, blossoming flower of death.

He was making a journey through the interior on his man-carrying pig, from Mataiea to Hitia'a, when he stopped in Faaone to take rest. Your mother asked him why he was going there, and he told her he was looking for a wife. She said the girls are much prettier in Faaone, my girl the prettiest, and he met her eyes boldly with his own then asked if she would like a husband for her girl! He wanted to know how old you were. She replied, old enough. You have no flower in your hair. Here is mine.

Tomorrow, you must place your flower behind the right ear, because you are taken. Don't worry, little sister, it will hurt at first, then it will get better, and you will surely enjoy it!

I watch them from the other side of the square. They wait in a row like fruit on a shelf, mango, guava, papaya, their black seeds spilling.

The girl in green exhales, a ring of smoke dancing upwards, it disappears into the sea, which lies between the trees. She gives her cigarette to the girl in red, whose brow glistens with sweat, dark circles around her armpits. Her dress has been sewn tight to show off every line and curve of her young body. The girl in yellow brings up a square of folded paper, and waves it over her face, eyes darting, searching. Searching.

They wait in a row, the girls on the bench, their bare feet rubbing the earth, a long shadow in the place where the grass once grew. The fishermen have strung out their morning catch and are close enough for us to hear, their words cast out towards the girls, in the way they fling their nets into the water.

The meat market has a fine selection today!

The girl in yellow folds her piece of paper into a smaller square and gets up now, like a bird from a nest of eggs. She walks calmly to the edge of the road where The Gendarme waits, but before she can reach him, he turns towards the big house, its arched windows peering over the tall fence. She follows him, the girl in yellow, pushing her way through the gate, where his wife usually stands, and climbs the front steps in two strides, disappearing through the opening, which swallows her whole.

I want to ask, what is written on that piece of paper she has tucked into the collar of her dress?

How much?

A white woman leans over us, pointing to one of Foster Mother's fans and her husband, The Official, quickly scoops it up. They inspect her work carefully, taking it in turns to wave the fan over their faces, hitting it gently against the palm of the hand to test its strength. After some consideration, the woman nods in approval, and her *tane* asks again, how much?

His shoes are black, shinier than the dome of Foster Mother's head when I've rubbed it with *monoi* under the noonday sun. I can see my face in them, these instruments that keep the white man's feet from touching the ground. I can't see the market place, or the girl in the yellow, or the silvery skin of the *tunny* fish, can't hear the breath of the girl in green, or the fishermen who quietly laugh, but I can hear The Missionary. He stands beneath the shade of the *pandanus*, watching the girls, his cross winking like the sun on the river as he rubs the body of his god's son between his fingers, his mouth moving in prayer.

She drops two coins into the skirt of my dress, The Official's Wife, and I hand it over to my Foster Mother whose eager palm is ready and waiting. The creases across her brow disappear for a moment, as they turn their backs on us, our first and last customers of the day. Contented with their purchase, they head towards the fishermen, who jump up eagerly to receive them, smiles erasing their sour expressions. There are empty shadows beneath the *pandanus* where The Missionary stood, moments ago, offering his prayer for the girls, now women.

Knowledge is like ivy, it grows quickly, and clings to everything. This is what the women say, once girls.

Once, a long time ago, the men launched their dugouts from the black sand. Once, she lay in her Foster Mother's arms, her thoughts not fully formed.

The girl in the painting is a woman now, powerless, powerful. Deadly. She is death and she is life. Her life creaks, like the hull of a ship that's moved across the oceans and the continents, too many times to count.

Her flesh creaks, because she's also made of wood, though from another kind of tree. She whispers, help me, but it's a question, not a plea, and her whisper becomes the hush of the sea.

Waves envelop her.

The painting lies in the hold, inches from a dead whale, which languishes in a shallow pool of saltwater. The iron smell of black-red blood fills the air. Protected by sackcloth, and secured with coconut twine, she is finally leaving her birthplace.

Foster Mother carries the girl's broken body from the belly of the ship, onto the deck, towards the bow, where she opens her eyes to glimpse an infinite palace of nails that were treasures once. Foster mother will tell her a story, because she has asked for one, demanded it, and she will listen with heart intact, to the story of the house of wooden images. She will see, in her mind's eye, the priest who made them, and how he carved them, made them walk, made them dance.

The ship floats, steers silently, moving across the endless empty seas, for days, weeks, years, a century, and a half, until one day, it finally reaches its stop.

She will find herself at the opposite end of the trajectory from where she began. And yet, she never left Tahiti.

Dear Diary,

This morning, I was lying in bed when I heard the sound of a carriage coming to a halt in the street below, and our family name being called out. I threw off my covers and rushed to the window to see two hefty Danes easing down a large parcel from the roof rack. One of them disappeared inside with it. Still in my nightdress, I ran down the stairs two at a time and almost fell headlong into the package, which was wrapped in sackcloth and secured with rope. I knew immediately it was from Papa, all the way from Tahiti.

It was addressed to Maman, the large thick lettering drawn in black paint. Maman pushed me aside with irritation and told the man to position it against the far wall, then reluctantly gave him fifty kroner, as is the custom here. When he was gone, she told P to fetch a knife with which to cut the rope but he ignored her request, so I ran to the kitchen to fetch one myself.

What a sight it is to behold! Mormor calls it disgusting, but Papa claims it is his best work yet. He says it will rival Manet's very own Olympia, and proclaims the girl in the painting, a Savage Eve, a Black Venus who belongs to a Paradise Lost.

The painting is of a native lying on her front, her face turned to the viewer, a cloaked figure crouching at the foot of the bed. Papa calls it The Spirit of the Dead Keeps Watch and gave an explanation in his letter so Maman will know the story behind the picture and what to say to the critics when the time comes. He wants Maman to take it to Paris where he says it will be the star of the show upon his return!

Mormor proclaims Papa mad. She says Maman will not leave everything behind in order to organise an exhibit, which she is certain will be a disaster if this is to be the centerpiece.

Maman has turned the painting to the wall so we do not have to feast our eyes on The Abomination.

In his description, Papa explains she is terrified of the dark, this girl; that all the people on the island sleep with a lamp burning beside the door, in order to keep out the ghosts. They call them *tupapau* (the spirits of the dead), and the title of the painting in their language is *Manao Tupapau*. This is what Papa will call it. The translation is merely for our benefit. I copied it into the palm of my hand so I could transfer it to my diary. A whole sentence condensed in two words, what a strange and marvelous thing!

Apparently, the girl entered his hut and took off her dress, as one discards rotten fruit. It is why she is naked. How can she be so fearless, and free? And that is Maman's pillowcase she rests her head upon, the edges of which are embroidered with rosebuds and their tiny leaves. I clearly remember watching her sew them. I threaded the very needle.

Papa says he has put a streak of fear in the girl's eyes. She lies belly down, the palms of her hands pressed firmly on the pillow, as though waiting for something, or someone. The idea is that she is about to have intercourse, or has just had it – both stories answer well to her character. Maman did not convey these details to me but I know of them because I found Papa's letter on her dresser. I memorised every word.

Did she really tell him she had just had intercourse? Does she know he has put the figure of the death inside the room, at the bottom of the bed, and not outside where she thinks it must be?

We are lucky, sighs Foster Mother. You are mine, and I am yours, and she gives the girl a new name on entering her own hut, a short distance from Birth Mother's. Through the long grass she had gone, and over the damp earth, leaving behind the imprint of her impatient feet.

Relief washes over her.

She lays the child down, this living gift, with sure hands, and unwraps it with all the tenderness of a proud mother, with trepidation, and the utmost reverence. She tells the girl the meaning of the name she has bestowed upon her: the giver of strength, or, the one who carries strength.

The child peers back at her, a frown line forming between the eyes, which seem unsettled, almost tearful. She gently rubs the offending expression away, shaking her head, smiling inside, and the girl responds by letting out a long cry of frustration, or is it hunger? Foster Mother yanks up her threadbare dress, and pushes the dark plum nipple of one humungous breast into her child's mouth. She is completely naked beneath the white man's cloth but who is there to see?

She lives all alone. At night, she sleeps with just a *pareu* covering her nut-brown skin.

Outside, the clouds hurry across the sky, masking then revealing the sun, in a game of hide and seek.

A cockerel crows, a bird calls, an indecipherable song, a dog howls, then another, and another, while inside, the child suckles, noisily, blissfully, finally stilling herself. Silence eventually reigns. Everywhere.

In time, a drumbeat begins, a murmur. Moving out from the interior, joining the breath of the sea, that great moving *marae*, which speaks of grief, and memory, and separation.

The ocean throws itself up against the island's *makatea*, again and again, but the reef holds it back with a greater strength.

Foster Mother's gaze falls on The Gospel, its presence at that moment disturbing her peaceful idyll. She rises quickly to clasp it in her free hand, and slides it beneath her mat. The Good Book has shared her life these many years, and like a lover, has slept beside her, its stories a source of wonder in the depths of her slumber. But too many times she has woken, to the grasp of invisible hands tightening around her neck, and now she will not sleep without the flame of her old belief burning securely in the doorway.

She has been faithful to the teachings of the white man, has never once missed his call to prayer, her sturdy feet moving swiftly to the sharp sound of the bell. She still remembers the day they arrived, the men. They entered her village in their strange clothes, bearing black books as gifts, their skin whiter than their teeth, and their voices softer than the birds in the trees that day.

Since that day, which she had been waiting for, she has kept her body firmly within The True Path, but now.

Now, she informs her child, I want to tell you about the world and how it was truly made.

Dear Diary,

When I look upon The Little One is Dreaming, I feel a great sadness take hold, and what I remember of those moments are now lost forever. I am lying in my cot clasping my blue blanket to me, to my chin, with my two little fists, which cannot be seen, because I am turned to the wall, fast asleep, just the backs of my legs showing, my left ear pink with heat. I can see the side of my face, my jowly cheek, and my shorn brown hair. I am facing the dark oak panels, and Papa is painting me without my knowledge.

He has set himself up in my room after I have fallen asleep. He has carried up a newly stretched canvas, his easel, a jar of brushes, and another of turpentine. My favorite toy, Mr. Clown, with his red topcoat and pointy hat, lost on the way from Paris to Copenhagen, hangs from the curved iron railing of my cot. How I cried, not for Mr. Clown, but for Papa, who was left behind with C. Why, I asked Maman, why not me? Because he is the youngest and needs his Papa, she said. But really, I know Papa wanted to keep one of us with him and Maman wouldn't let him have me. Then, later, she went back to Paris to fetch C after Papa sent word he had taken ill. He got better when he came home but was a different boy, quieter, with angry eyes. He never spoke about his year with Papa "in a garret shut up on his own while his Papa went out to get drunk with his artist-friends", Mormor once revealed.

Papa paints black birds in the wallpaper above my head, their wings outstretched in a green sky, though they do not exist. No, they do not. He is making it as though I am dreaming of them. In truth, I wish I could be one of those birds. I would fly all the way to Tahiti and land right there beside him, to know what she really looks like, because from here, I can only see one side of her face, and that uncouth mouth pressed to Maman's pillow, the audacity of her naked stance. Am I jealous? I fear I am.

Truly. Of Papa's muse, because that is what she is. She has all his love now, my Papa, and she is everything I am not, and more.

In the depths of night, when I am sure everyone is asleep, and the house plunged into darkness, with just the ticking hands of the clock on the stair, I make my way to where she lies, facing the wall. I turn her around and crouch there, shivering in the cold, beside the lamplight. I look, and look, but I cannot know her thoughts, however hard I try. What lies behind that brow? What does she see from that one exposed eye? Does her heart beat as wildly mine?

It is like she is whispering to me from across the oceans. Does she know the earth is round, and we are all held in place by a magnetic force? Something connects me to her, and it is not just Papa. She does not speak but her look does, her body a landscape of glory.

She is more beautiful than Manet's Olympia, more powerful in a way. Yes, Papa has created something truly magnificent with this new piece of work, and the knowledge fills me with fear, and with confusion. And because of that, I wish her dead. I know it is wrong.

I have these feelings I am not proud of. I want to be good, to love what Papa loves and yet, I cannot. I am scared. Scared he will love her more than me and he will forget my promise.

You came into my hut to set me free. I did not know it then, but I was already free. Free when you pushed back the gates to the interior.

I used to imagine I was trapped like the vini bird, held in a cage of bamboo reed, my blood red feathers stolen, and tied to the wooden gods on the *marae*. Tied to the cloaks of the *Areois* and the headdresses of the priests, and chiefs. They used to hunt them, the vini. They scaled the mountains for them, until they were all lost.

But I am not that sacred. Hiding, trembling at the sound of human feet on fallen leaves.

And I nod. I nodded, like a bird trapped and taught to bend. I said yes. I did not hear the trees just beyond the opening, whispering, or the waves even further still, sighing. I did not look up before I went back into my Foster Mother's hut. I forgot to glimpse once again, my *fenua*, rising up towards a sky made of hard rock crystal. I did not realise it then, but I was free from the moment of my birth, even before you came, to set me free.

I did not realise it then, but we are not of the same trunk, as the wise men once predicted. They said that you would come, those of your kind, colour and cloth, to conquer and make this land your own. Even then, afterwards, I was free, born here in this village of Faaone, hidden from you, until you pushed back the gates, and decided to go further, to the other side of the island, to find yourself a wife. Even then, I was grateful.

Are you disappointed?

My landlord built that house over there to rent out to white men like me, but I preferred this. If I had told you I lived in a hut, would you have come? Would your mother have let you go, both of them? I love you.

Don't worry, you can tell me when you're ready. We have time. All the time there is.

Your hut is the same as the one I grew up in, but not the same. The walls have openings that look out onto your world, and in each, there is a woman who seems to me, beautiful, brave and free. Above your doorway, one of them lies naked, her skin pale as bark cloth before it is dyed, a black ribbon tied around the neck, with shoes that hide her toes but not the heels, one hand covering her sex.

A woman stands in a wide green lake, a white-feathered duck floating before her, its neck as long as her arm. A woman lies on a cliff top, blood red fields below her. She holds a sharp-eyed creature on her shoulder, its paw between her breasts. In a yellow field, three girls dance, their hair hidden under strange-looking hats, a bright flower pinned to a dark dress. One girl pulls away. Three men set off with a pack of dogs, or are they returning? Their world is covered in white, from the top of the mountains to the bottom of the valley where the people look like insects.

Against the far wall stands a bed, a proper bed, one made of wood with legs that keep it off the ground. The first thing you do, is take my parcel from me, and untie it. The next thing you say is, you won't need this here, then you place The Good Book on a high shelf beside a dark green bottle, the mango beneath it, between tins of food and half a loaf of bread. You lay my *pareu* on your bed, the palm of your hand flat on a leaf, a finger tracing a stalk. There's no oil for your lamp, you say, but tomorrow I'll buy some.

I want to ask, tomorrow, will you close the windows, which look out onto the world beyond?

Take off your dress.
I want to look at you, you say. Just look.

47

She unclenches one fist, then another, allowing her dress to fall to the floor.

She presses the palms of her hands flat against her thighs. That is the cloth they wrapped me in, she thinks, when I was born, the one, which now covers his bed. Her chest tightens.

It's as though Foster Mother is pulling the last long *pandanu* leaf through the border of one of her intricate fans, which will be stained with the colour of edible mountain berries.

Once he has looked at her, like a woman choosing a piece of fish, from the crown of her head, to the tips of her toes, even asking her turn in a circle so he can study the back of her, he tells her to put her dress back on. He closes his eyes, letting out a small sigh then rises to light a candle, driving its end into the earth beside her abandoned lamp. To keep out your ghosts, he says, with a half-smile.

She's seen that look before – like they own the world. She knew the world was bigger than Faaone, and wider, full of secrets, and she had wanted to know them, every single one.

On the first night, he takes her by the hand and leads her to the bed, their bed, but not to do what he promised himself he will not do. I will not touch, he'd told himself, over and over, again and again, until his mantra merged with the sound of the sea, and the wheels of the trap moving across stony ground towards Mataiea.

I will not touch, not tonight, not just yet. But now, he cannot contain himself inside that noble promise. He kisses the flat tip of her nose, the faintly drawn brows, and the full mouth, boldly pushing his tongue between her lips, her clenched teeth. She submits.

He clings to her, breath buried against skin, and consumes the sweet-bitter scent, gets drunk on it, but the spirit of her eludes him. Soon, he says, soon, not to her, but to his wounded ego, and takes comfort in the fact, in the eventuality, the certainty of their consummation. It had been a foolish fantasy when he'd borrowed The Official's horse and made his way through the interior, looking for a wife.

She can hear his heart knocking against his chest, like the flutter of a wing against a wall, a bird inside in a box, she thinks. She strains from him, to take a few gulps of the hot night air, knowing what will come next. Foster Mother had told it her when she was young, one evening as the rain fell softly on their *pandanu* leaf roof, when the world was completely dark, but still safe. They were lying beside one another, Teha'amana and her *metua tavai*, curled up on their mat like stacked gourds, which were living things once, pith and flesh scooped out and dried under the sun to harden. She plunges the moment from her mind.

She sees a face, hers, in shadow through a hole. The window of a ship. Then this image too disappears.

Now she sees the *Areois* women, standing outside the walls of his hut, with their hands drawn up at their ears, listening with their entire bodies.

Like the wooden images that entered the priest's house and were taught to dance, the ancient priest who made them from *toromiro* wood blackened by the flames of a fire, then brought them to life.

Each of her thoughts trembles now, like the long lips of a hibiscus flower, dark, dark pink. He gathers up the skirt of her dress in both hands, then pushes two fingers through the hair between her legs, to that secret, sacred place.

She submits.

Once upon a time, the world was a dark, infinite void. There were no ends to the earth or the sky, no parts to the day. There was no moon, no sun, nor a single star.

A shell turned in that never-ending blackness, revolving, spinning, egg-shaped, and enclosed within, was Ta'aroa. He lived alone, mother and father to himself, the first spirit, being, and thought.

One day, bored with his own company, he decided to unfold himself, and flicked open his shell with his wings, which were of red, yellow, green, and blue feathers. Unveiling the fierceness of his beauty, he looked out into the world beyond with a penetrating gaze, and his first words were, is anyone there? But there was no answer. Hey, ho, he shouted, is there anyone above? Then again, is anyone below? But all that came back to him was the echo of his own voice. So, in anger, he rose up, lengthening his spine, and split open his shell so it became two halves, one half of which he balanced in the palm of his left wing.

He called out once more, is anyone behind? Is anyone in front? But nothing and no one answered or obeyed him. Now, with his anger bubbling forth like lava from a volcano, he shook his thick matted locks, and raised one half of his upturned shell to make the dome of the sky. With the other half, which he had stepped out of, he fixed the foundation of the earth.

Then, Ta'aroa gave his backbone for a mountain range, he took his ribs for the ridges that ascend, his flesh for the abundance of the earth, and his legs and arms for the strength of that newly formed terrain. With his tears he nourished the valleys, and with his toenails and fingernails, he created the fish in the lakes, and the rivers. His guts, he gave for all the slithering, and creeping things in the water, and his innards he took to make the clouds in the sky, which floated away. And with his colourful feathers he clothed the land with shrubs, trees, flowers, and the many, varied grasses.

Why did you do that?

You would not wake, though I called your name a great many times, the sun is high and I must begin my work.

But it's too early!

The early bird catches the worm.

She wipes the water from her face, then slowly, and reluctantly, props herself up against the pillows.

He waits, irritation mounting. Then gently places the pewter tankard in her lap, the tankard, which was once filled with malt beer, and now with steaming hot tea.

Remorsefully, he attempts to dab away the droplets on her nose with the edge of her *pareu*, but she shakes him off grumpily, still sluggish with sleep. He sits back on his heels, impatient, bristling, hoping she'll not fly into another tantrum.

She'd seemed wise beyond her years. When I first laid my eyes upon her, I was sure she'd make a good model, but now, he thinks, I'm not certain.

With a sigh, she gives in, fixing her gaze on the ugly drinking vessel. It's like nothing she's ever seen before. She lifts it up, clicks open the lid, and takes a sip of the white man's tea. Always too sweet, she screws up her face in disgust. That face, he thinks, with a sudden affection, but turns away, does not want to indulge her at this moment. The sun is high, and the light a perfect slant through the doorway, the shadows lively. He takes the six steps required to reach the other side, where the canvas awaits. This, he'd told her, is where I do my work, and you must not touch anything in this part of the hut, do you understand?

She'd replied by saying nothing. She closes her eyes now, and takes another sip of his tea, wincing.

With his blood still simmering, he disappeared, Ta'aroa, to become all that is red in the world, the sky at dawn, at dusk, the red of the rainbow, and the flower of the flamboyant, the feathers of the vini bird. But his head, his head remained sacred, and it became tapu.

Silence encompassed the darkness of Havaiki, the birthplace of Ta'aroa, where he once existed in his fullness, and yet he had not been alone. She had also prevailed, his helper. And her name was Hina.

On the silt bed of Lake Vaihiria, where the water springs and runs, she now resides, in the liquid heart of the island. From above, the lake looks like a giant hand mirror, with the entire valley caught inside it. The forests on the mountains fall inwards towards another sky.

Once, a long time ago, she jumped into that lake, when the four pillars that held up the world refused her request. She had asked them, in turn, who her father was. And with their muteness, came her answer.

He stands by the glistening waters of the lake, summoning her, calling for her return, but she denies him with just one word. Then other words come.

I will remain in Po, in the eternal dark, carrying our secret, and I will drag our children down when their time comes on earth. This world I helped you create, O Father.

She became then Hina-nui-te-Po, the Great Goddess of Darkness – silence her true companion.

How do you make human beings with colour?

The correct word for that is Painter. I am a painter. I paint them, human beings. But I like how you describe it. I like it very much.

What is paint?

Look. See this? They contain the most important colours, magenta, cyan blue and yellow. All other colours come from them. They are dust of stone pigment ground down. I will mix them with oil from these jars to make the colour of your skin.

I am the colour of the earth.

The earth has many shades. You are burnt umber here on this bed with only the moon for light, and beneath the sun, beyond these walls, you are yellow ochre, my dear Teha'amana.

One day, you will not want to lie down beside me, your mother. You will not demand a story to make you fall asleep. You will share your mat with your *tane*, and if you are lucky, it will be a bed with good dreams. And you will ask him to do what men do, with your eyes wide open.

It is like a drink of water, sex. Like kneeling beside the river and drinking 'til you've had your fill, simple as that. It is not something to be dwelt on, but lived in.

Inseparable took her twin brother's hand and climbed through the window into the ink-black night.

The smoke from the earth oven rose up towards a sky where the moon sat, perfectly round. Their mother was roasting the bony red, which was wrapped in pandanu leaves, a delicious feast for their father. The smell of the fish cooking had seeped in through the gaps between the walls of their hut and woken them and they had lain there, on their mats, hunger clawing at their bellies. Earlier, they had eaten a simple meal of baked uru.

They crossed the lagoon now, Inseparable and her twin-brother, the rock floor cutting their feet, but they did not yield. They crouched in the water gripping the corners of their fishing net. Soon, we will build a fire in the sand dunes with driftwood and coconut husk, and we will fill our bellies, Inseparable told her brother, and he nodded in excitement, shivering with cold. But their net did not pull, and the sea grew wild, crashing up against the reef, finally pushing them back in defeat.

They heard their mother's cry from the shore, calling them home in anger. So they ran from her again, out of the lagoon, towards the peak of Arorai, ascending the mountain ladder up into the night.

With each step they took, they heard their mother nearing, but they carried on climbing without stopping for even a moment. When they finally reached the summit, Inseparable took her twin-brother's hand and held it tight. She told him, don't worry. I'll always be near, beside you, forever.

Then she tugged him quick into the black roof of the sky, just before their mother could catch them.

Now, every night, they shine side by side, keeping the moon company, as it blooms into a full circle then falls away, until it becomes a fingernail, a shard.

I will not question my good fortune. God has been kind, if indeed he exists. Now drink up, you'll sleep well after a few sips, not that you need much help in that regard, a girl who snores, and sleeps like an armadillo!

Have you been with another? A nice Tahitian boy perhaps, one with big strong arms and smoldering eyes. I've heard how easy it is, that it takes just one look, and off you go into the bushes, the boy following the girl, not the other way around… drink, you'll soon like the way it warms the belly and slows the blood.

I think I've finally made good progress and there are enough studies here for the painting I have in mind. Yes, I am content with what I have achieved today. It's a shame I couldn't reward you with a feast, but your mother's mango was tasty, was it not?

Succulent.

Drink, I'll pick up another bottle from the Chinaman in Taravao, and put it on credit until my money arrives, and it will. No, I won't forget the oil for your lamp, and if I see your mother, I'll tell her you're happy. Is that not correct?

You are my wife now, and the past means nothing. My life began the day you walked through the door with the light crowning your perfect form. Did you know I thought you more beautiful than Botticelli's Venus arriving at the shore, already a woman at birth?

No, I'm not sorry, not sorry at all.

I'm not like the girls in the market place, in the village, on the wooden bench. I am not like them.

I'm not like the girls in the dugout canoes, rowed by their fathers across the water to meet the first white men. I'm not like them. Who am I then?

I am the girl who lies on your bed so you can make her in one day, who feels sadness when the sun goes away, who crawls to you like a spider to its web, who drinks absinthe because it is better than mending nets for a fisherman. I am the girl who takes off her dress again, so you can make her, but this time not with colour, while holding my Foster Mother's mango.

I lie down beside you, beneath you, above, but never inside, with my legs wide, and my eyes open. It is you. You penetrate the very flesh of me, open me like a blunt knife through ripe fruit. And beyond these walls, beyond the road carved into our island, beyond the lagoon, the waves still crash. And where the *makatea* does not protect, the ocean enters and mixes with the clear waters of the blue.

Afterwards, you hold me to you, pressing your words to my hair, and ask if it is true, the story of offerings to the great god Ta'arao. And you tell it me, because I do not say yes, I do not say no.

Once, long ago, there was a drought. The land was withering, and the people were dying. We gave many offerings to Ta'aroa, of fish, but the rains refused to come. The priests then said we must give something more powerful, and quake before Ta'arao. So, we gave him the first man, and the rains, they came. We realised he preferred human flesh, and his son Oro, he liked it better, the flesh of men, whom we called long-legged fish. Is that not true, you ask?

Dear Diary,

I sat contemplating the moment that brought me here. The seat was hard as usual, and the atmosphere, dim and depressing. The only thing divine about the place was its stained glass window, which stood tall as a doorway behind the central altar, now alive with the afternoon light.

Our Savior was making his final journey through the streets, his torso bruised and battered, his back bowed down by the weight of the cross he would die upon. Behind him, the men in power followed in their robes of velvet, and crowns of gold, and with spears and shields they prodded him. Angels wept, hovering with dragonfly wings, whilst Mary clung to him, a black cloth covering her hair, face pinched with grief. As I sat there, contemplating the scene, I remembered Papa's ode to sacrifice and how nothing good ever comes of it.

As soon as I saw the priest enter the confessional, I went quickly towards it, my heart hammering against my ribcage. Inside, behind the grill, heavy boots scraped against wood, and after a few moments, a gruff voice asked – what would you like forgiveness for, my child?

I had not uttered a single word. How could he know?

I listened to the long uneven breath for what seemed like minutes, but was merely seconds. I could make out his hunched form through the ornate ironwork, and without further ado, plucking up all the courage in my innocent breast, surprising even myself, I told him what I had done. I had wanted to be like her, bold, monstrous, and free. Though I did not tell him that. Then I would have had to explain all about Papa and Tahiti and The Painting. So, I began my story when I entered the forest, earlier.

The dark fir trees stood, unmoving, shielding me from a lake peopled with swans, and beneath the ravens' cries, I took off my dress, my stockings, and my chemise. It was an exhilarating feeling, though my body shook with fear. I felt light headed and dizzy, so I crouched down for a moment into a tight ball then lay back against a bed of needles, which pricked my back, but I did not care. I looked up through the crown of the trees towards the clouds, digging my fingers into the earth. It felt as though the world was going to tip over.

Eventually, the loud thumping in my heart subsided and sweet still air warmed my skin, my limbs, which had been hidden for so long.

The priest breathed a wordless response, and I loathed him for it. He reminded me of the black oxen at the farmers' fair in Toulouse that Papa once took us to. They had breathed the same way, and with their dark eyes gleaming, I knew if I'd stepped into the enclosure, they would tear me to pieces. So I ran out of the box of secrets, past Christ bearing his cross in glass, out of those heavy wooden doors, back home to Maman, and you, my Dear Diary.

She looks at me with pity, watches me from the corner of her eye, with mistrust, with a smirk, with sorrow, or is it victory? She possesses a world that will always be, beyond my grasp, but most of all, she has laid claim to my Papa, with her body, which is that of a woman's, not a child.

Her presence weighs heavy on this house. She has become an unwelcome addition to our family, a living thing who shares these walls now.

She squatted in the sand and gave birth. Not to a child, but to an egg. Then, she cut the cord with the sharpened edge of a bamboo reed, dug a hole, and buried her secret in haste, and in confusion.

Later, as she lay beside her tane, racked with guilt, she told him what she had done.

So, they hurried, these two, under the cover of night to unearth the egg, which was the size of a large rock. They carried it to a secluded cave by the sea, close to the reef, where only the distant thunder of the surf could be heard and the long cry of the terns. There, they kept a fearful vigil for one whole week, until a fine crack appeared on surface of the shell. Finally, a boy's head poked through, but he possessed the body of a mo'o, green, pale gray, blue-dark, with hints of yellow. Huge round tears fell from the eyes of the lizard boy when he saw the horror on his parents' faces, and his mother, now full of remorse, took the child in her arms. They kept him there, in the cave, and promised to return everyday with food, with whatever they could find, fetch, hunt, fish, and pluck.

Such was his appetite he soon grew strong, equaling the size of a horse, an animal that had never been seen before on the island, until the advent of the white man. As a consequence, his parents had less to eat and some days they only had one piece of fruit to share between them. But his mother had made a promise, something tapu, never to be broken, never to be motu. I will feed you, my son, always, she said. And I will protect you, my mother, he replied. Such was their bond. Days went by. The lizard boy grew, and so did his appetite.

He was a talented child. He could suspend himself from the roof of his cave with feet that possessed three hundred hooks on each sole, and he had clear secondary lids, which meant he could keep his eyes shut yet be watchful at the same time. His tongue was as long as his strong body and could be propelled in a flash to catch any living thing that strayed too far, and he could hear all the way to the foot of mountains, to the creeks where human beings had made their homes. In this way, he listened in to their *conversations, heard them outside their doorways, contemplating their food stores, the taro harvest that year, or if Ruahatu, the sea god, had been kind. He clung, the lizard boy, to the slippery rock, hidden, with all his senses open. He listened for his sweet mother's voice, as she whispered to his father, about what they would bring their son later that day. And he heard this.*

I am tired of having to constantly feed him. He eats so much. He's getting much too big to stay hidden in the cave forever. If he were a pig, at least, we could kill him and roast him! We ourselves are going hungry to satisfy his needs.

He was deeply hurt, the lizard boy, the product of a man and a woman. So hurt was he, the pain dug clean into his human heart, and tore it in two, and he fell, crashing to the rock floor, then crawled out, dazed into the bright light of day. He looked to his left, and to his right, the saltwater lapped on either side, beyond an empty stretch of sand.

He slithered across the lagoon and climbed up onto the reef, scuttling all the way along it with the sea crashing at his feet. He turned once to look inland, and there were many people gathered, running towards the shore. They thought a giant monster had risen out of the sea, and his mother and father were also there amongst them. They stood in silence, not once did they call out to their son. Turning away, in grief, and anger, he jumped into the sea, swimming towards the open waves. With the current lashing on all sides, it overwhelmed him, or it is said, he gave up.

His jagged lizard body floated up to the surface, his head hidden beneath the water, and he turned into an island.

He became the mountainous landscape of Mo'orea, yellow-green, gray shadowed, and midnight blue. Today, the peaks of Mo'orea rise up towards the sky. Sometimes the clouds cover them, just as they cover the moon.

I want these.

But they're made from copper.

I like them.

I'm not paying ten francs for some cheap rubbish; these fellows are very clever, going around selling trinkets for a song, targeting the likes of us.

But all the girls are wearing them.

Why do you want to be like other girls?

I want these!

As I told you, I am going to Taravao today, and I will spend ten francs on oil for your lamp, and food – you will eat like a queen tonight, no more bread and corned beef, how about that?

Taneipa, can you hear it, she's beating her *tapa* on the moon?

No, but I can see him, Ta'aroa, his crater-like eyes, flared nostrils, a dimple in his chin.

Ta'aroa killed Hina with her own mallet and her spirit flew up to the moon where she still beats *tapa*.

Ta'aroa kept his head for himself, that's why it's up there, in the night sky, out of reach.

The noise was keeping him awake.

Which god do you believe in, theirs or ours?

Theirs is ours.

They put their own god to death, little sister.

Earlier, she'd built a fire outside their hut to cook the fish he had brought back with him, keeping a portion of it for herself, to eat raw. Now, he opens another bottle of absinthe for the occasion of their parting, and they pass it between them, until both are quite inebriated. Finally, a smile softens her serious countenance, which is rather disconcerting for one so young. She casts her eyes up towards me hanging above the doorway and bold with drink, asks if I am his true wife. He laughs at her assumption. Humiliated, she snatches the bottle back, taking another lengthy sip.

A petal from the flower Édouard placed behind my ear falls suddenly onto the edge of my bed, brushing my arm. I am not sure if she notices, but the woman in my room does, the one with dark-black skin who hovers, an irrepressible shadow at my feet, the white-yellow of her eyes gleaming. I refuse to acknowledge her presence even though she holds a sweet-smelling garland of posies for my benefit. I have trained myself to look straight ahead, below, and in front, at the events unfolding, while my ankles remain folded, one over the other. Cream backless slippers cover these feet that men have caressed, including Lautrec, Baudelaire, and Monet, to name a few.

He asks her to tell him a legend, a myth, which belongs to her people, her person. But she insists she knows none, says it with wide, innocent eyes. He looks into that face, uncompromising and beautiful, and forgives, though feeling somewhat cheated.

He crawls from their bed now, naked, and takes a small iron key from the pocket of his embroidered waistcoat, which was brightly coloured when he made its purchase at a market stall in Brittany. He has worn it every day, as a talisman, when he began to follow his true vocation. He certainly wore it every time he came to see me.

He unlocks the old wooden trunk that has travelled with him from Paris to Copenhagen, then on to Arles where poor Vincent met his fate, and Le Pouldu, where he told me he was the happiest. He takes from it, a green leather-bound tome, entitled

Voyage Aux Iles du Grand Ocean. From it he has managed to glean some of her myths and legends, and places it upon her lap, an offering, which she hesitantly accepts. She traces the curved gold lettering, touches the stretched, green-dyed cowhide cover with apprehension, but does not open it. She cannot read the name of the man who has written it. But I can. It is Jacques-Antoine Moerenhout.

The night air stifles and the mountains beyond are dark battlements, impenetrable, rising up towards the stars. The moon is not the only flame that lights their room this evening. Her lamp is finally lit. And he, crumpled and sorry, a Don Quixote three times her age, moves forward like a cat towards its prey, which remains fearfully still in order to save its own life.

He tells her again he loves her but she does not give him the answer he craves, her eyes fixed on the glowing lamp.

Impatient, he turns her face towards his, telling her he will be bereft when she is gone, and will mourn her absence until her return.

How long will you be gone, he whimpers.

But she keeps her cards hidden. She answers by pressing her eyelids shut and falling back, hoisting up the skirt of her dress.

She knows what he wants, and imagines it will be the last time.

His armpits smell.

Encourage him to bathe in the morning and the evening then rub his skin with *monoi.*

He's old.

Wisdom makes a man more powerful than ten strong young men.

All we eat is tinned meat.

Then gather fresh fruit, and catch shrimp in the pools, like I taught you.

He lives in a hut no bigger than ours.

I know.

How?

News travels fast, they say he prefers to live like us, but he is known in France, a big man.

He scratches all the time, like a dog with fleas.

Don't you want to go further than this place?

Until he bleeds.

We don't go inside, don't dare. We imagine we'll never be lucky enough to taste those things, the food held within. The shopkeeper sleeps sitting up, arms folded. All of sudden, he'll meet our eyes. He'll keep on looking, with mistrust, waiting for us to turn our backs. She'll pull me away first, reminding me our food is tastier, because it is fresh. Caught, plucked and cooked with our own bare hands.

Now she pulls away from me, and names the tins and boxes stacked across her shelf. Once, she fed me, carried me in her arms to her breast. Eat, she says, and offers me a pale gold biscuit from inside a big round tin. Eat!

It is sweet and crumbly and melts on the tongue. She closes her eyes joyfully, as she also eats of it. This *shortbread*, she says, comes all the way from Scotland, a country that lies beside England, and wars have been fought between the two over land and god, just like our clans. But she does not say, my Foster Mother, my *metua tavai* – until the white man made Pomare king.

She will not return my look, and draws the new sky blue cloth around her shoulders. As I reach out for it, she edges away, snatching the parcel from my lap. She unties it, and spreads it out across her mat, kneels over the gifts, picking up the dark blue ribbon, scooping the brass buttons into the palm of her other hand. Yes, those are for you, I tell her, and the white lace for Birth Mother, the rum for Father. This will go nicely with the dress I am making, she says.

Go now, your parents are waiting, it is the eighth day, and we will eat tender crab on your return, the dish you love best. I went out at first light, especially. We will make the most of our time together, before you return to your *tane*.

She carried me in her arms to her breast. Once, we built our nests in the branches of our mothers. It did not matter that mine was not my blood mother. It did not matter that I was dark, darker than her, because her wide hands held me, and her fearsome eyes kept me, closer still.

All the girls flew. Flapped their wings, one by one, flew towards the boys, and the men, and the thing which makes you free. That was my belief.

Uraave went out to fetch seawater for the coconut sauce that was fermenting, an accompaniment to the food her mother was preparing. The shrimp's head had already been stirred into the flesh of a young green coconut. So, Uraave took the large gourd that contained the sauce within it and made her way towards the lagoon. It cannot be fresh water, her mother reminded her.

Uraave stood with the bowl clasped in one arm where the water reached her ankles and turned to find her mother standing at the water's edge. She threw her question back over her shoulder. Is this a good place? No, her mother replied, go further. So she waded deeper, until the water reached her knees, where the current was unsettled, and clutching the bowl in one arm, she turned again, calling towards her mother. Can I fill it up now? But her mother replied, no, go a little further, then you will reach the salt water, and remember to rock it, the gourd, when you fill it.

So, Uraave went on, stepping lightly across the rock floor, and climbed up onto the ancient reef. She turned back to ask once more. But her mother did not answer, the cockerel did. It made a resounding cry, and she fell, Uraave, into the ocean, never to be seen again.

Today, a huge rock rises up through the waves, which the fishermen say is Uraave's resting place. Some dare climb it, and when they do, another boulder can be seen, in the depths, the shape of a bowl where the water swirls.

He makes me lie naked, makes me sit down on the floor of his hut, on a rock beside the river, in a forest clearing. Sometimes, he gets angry, and tells me to settle down, like I am a dog, or his child. He calls what he does *studies* or *preparations for the work* and makes me on pieces of paper or in the pages of a book.

When he is satisfied with what he has done, he'll send me away, to do as I please, but I must not go far, never too far. Then, I'll hide behind the trunk of a tree, or climb up between its branches, passing the time, looking for spiders. I'll abandon them far from their homes, or pluck worms from the ground and leave them in nests as gifts. From wherever I am, I can hear his mumbled anger as he taps out his colours, mixing them with oil from the jars. He is making a picture of me that's taking forever, which he says will be a *masterpiece*. In it, I'm lying naked on his bed, on my front, on Foster Mother's *pareu*, my head on his pillow.

But Taneipa is not listening. She takes my hand and guides it onto her belly, moving it in a small circle over the swell that's hidden beneath the loose cloth of her dress. She turns to me, eyes glinting, and nods at my silent question. She's more beautiful today than yesterday, than when she washed the blood from my tiny body.

The trees shiver as the breeze moves through them, and their leaves seem to also whisper, *Eha*!

Suddenly, she lets out a sharp whistle, and cranes her neck away from the river's edge where we are sitting, where we'd throw ourselves into the water and swim to the other side.

The shape of a young man emerges from behind a thicket. Taneipa squeezes my hand then releases it, places a quick kiss on top of my head, and runs toward the waiting figure. She turns once to raise her hand, before disappearing between the trunks of the trees. I want to tell her more, to tell her this.

I lie naked on my front, on the bed, on my *pareu*, my head on his pillow, facing the doorway, where she watches.

He calls her *my Olympia* but she was made by another white man who also makes human beings with colour.

Her eyes move in the darkness between the doorframe and the roof, her breasts rising, and falling with each breath. I've seen the flower in her hair break free, seen her reach down to pick it up with one small, graceful arm. She unties the black ribbon around her throat, and ties it back again into a bow. She does this at least three times a day. And when she yawns, she places a hand over her mouth, so that the palm faces outwards.

This is how women yawn, I imagine, in her world. The bracelet on her wrist makes a tinkling sound, like Sister striking the bell but far away on the other side of the island, from Faaone to Mataiea. Then I remember this is where I am, and how far I've come.

And she speaks to me, this Olympia, she says, I am amazed at your enduring ability to keep so very still. Are you not in the least bit bored? I shake my head in reply, because I want to appear strong. I tell her I am learning a lot, and this hut is more alive than the one I left behind.

But I am surprised, secretly. Secretly, I am *amazed* at my *enduring ability*, to *keep so very still*, for days, and days without end. I can't call this hut existence marriage or the real world, but a strange, strange dream.

What it must be, to hop grass, to balance on a shard of light, to be green and pure and hollow, to fall, kneel on your hind legs, to look up, and absorb every ounce of heat.

To perch on a high wall, a blade, a stair, the arm of a tree, to know and to understand, to enter the garden and not be ashamed.

It is said, is written, Man named each living thing, the dragonfly, hoverfly, yellow dung beetle, the slowworm, woodlouse, slug, wasp, ant. God brought them to him, but that was before.

He looked at them, Man, with intent, and plucked from his imagination the words that would name them, and make them known forever. And God, to reward such hard work, gave him a gift, took from his body, a bone, a meaningless one, then covered up the flesh and woke him from the deep.

Man named her, when she just a form, formless in her waking, but full of life and breath and wonder.

He called her Woman then gave her second name, but that was after.

She came to be known as Eve, because she would be his companion in everything, cling to him, mourn for him, and allow him to plant his seed in her. There were knives of flame guarding the way when the gates closed on them, Man and Woman, when their dream was lost. Taken, so it remains in the past, or the body of the past, and in that body, the grasshopper jumps, in silence, alone. She remembers looking up into the chamber of his eyes. Once, she believed, they held within them, all the fruits of gold.

Dear Diary,

Last night, I dreamt I was among the fir trees again, that I had stripped off, and my dress, shoes, and undergarments were nowhere to be seen. This time, however, my soul was free, and naked as my body, which was at one with the natural world. The ground beneath me was littered with needles and pinecones, but I did not care, and lay down upon them with relish.

A square had been cut from the dimly lit sky. It looked like a hatch door with white light pouring out of it. Instinctively, I rose to my feet, unsteady at first. I reached out to grasp the rung of an invisible ladder. I began to climb, moving slowly with hesitation, though my hands were firmly pulling me upwards. I could hear Papa's voice beneath the sound of water running into a bathtub, and I desperately needed to reach him, so I kept on climbing, rung after rung, while the water kept on gurgling. Then his voice disappeared, and I waked, before I could reach the top.

Unable to sleep, I decided to go up to the attic where Maman has banished *Manao Tupapau* – so it will not create any further disturbance. Out of sight is out of mind, she says, but I know she does not believe it. Now, I cannot look at her whenever I please, cannot turn her around to glimpse once again, Papa's private world, a little piece of Tahiti on my way to the kitchen, the dining room, to school, and back again, before bed.

Now, she lies directly above me, in the place that was Papa's painting room, beside his very own Self-Portrait in Front of the Easel. Sometimes, I imagine they speak to one another, from across their respective borders, separated by the space between them, when in real life, I know they are not. In real life, Papa reaches out to touch her, and I imagine he sweeps his fingers along the dip in her back and makes her shiver. In real life, she takes his hand, and turning herself over, places it in the crease between her legs.

The wooden floorboards announced my arrival with every creaking step. Maman has pushed the paintings up against the far wall, side by side, with just an inch between them, and in the flickering glow of my lamp, they seemed very much alive. It was as though they had just stopped conversing the moment the door handle turned.

She has laid claim to Papa's sacred space, where I have watched him work, where he allowed me to remain – as long as I was quiet. On the old mattress in the corner of the room, there he would lay, stretching himself out, crying with fatigue, and sometimes he would sleep like that, for days upon end. And I would lie beside him, for an hour or two, before Maman called me away, Papa's disappearances already an accepted thing by then.

She carried on looking at me through the lamplight, keeping her silence, in the way that she does with one eye hidden, and half her mouth concealed by an outstretched palm, which lies across Maman's pillowcase. I presented the back of my head to her steadfast gaze, barring her view of Papa. I required some time alone with him. Dear heart, I began, I had a bad dream, I was climbing and it was going on forever.

I was trying to reach the clouds, because it looked like there was an opening in the sky.

It was just a dream, he replied, don't fret now, Papa is here.

I could hear your voice coming from inside the bright light.

What was I saying?

You were telling me to look after Maman and not fight with C.

That is correct, you are the older by two years.

But today, he threw water over my dress and ran away.

I will speak to him, but you must not argue all the time.

He's infuriating.

You should be the one to set an example, and remember to always keep your love sacred.

What does that mean, I never did care to ask?

It is something holy and must be worshipped as such.

Like God?

Yes, just like that.

So we must keep our love like God?

Yes, my sweet.

But once, right here in this room, on that mattress, you told me you did not believe in God.

Sometimes you have to throw things away in order to realise their importance, my flower.

Like me?

Don't be silly, my darling. I never left, I'm right here.

Show me then, that you are, give me a sign.

Guilt fills her eyes, like a high mountain pool about to flow over.

Guilt shapes her smile, makes her strong hands tremble. I want to take them in my own, rub out the creases and swells, but I don't. Instead, I watch her every movement, the knowing tightening to a hard knot in my middle. She wraps the food between two coconut leaves, to take home with me. This is my home and yet…I am going back.

I watch as she fastens the knot once more, the edges of the *pareu*, dark blue and bright yellow.

It will be laid out on your bed when I return, like me. When I return, you will lay it out, spread it out like the roots of a tree, and you will place your hand on a leaf. Before you push yourself inside me, at dusk, like a bee.

The brick wall separates the white man's temple from the road. A long time ago, The Missionary laid the first foundation stone, after which he said, I am proud, I am very proud, these bricks travelled with me all the way from France. I was just a child then, clinging to my Foster Mother's legs, which were hidden under the flowing cloth of her new dress. She led me towards the villagers gathered before The Missionary then we followed him through the door, and sat down on long wooden benches, the men on one side, and the women on the other, our gaze turned towards the man on the cross. Our eyes pinned to the violence of this new religion.

But it is locked now, the door through which I have walked many times, freely, and I know she is watching, my Foster Mother, on the other side of the road, anxious to see what I'll do next. I make my way around the side of the church, along its thick white walls, knowing she'll be following closely behind. I run towards the House of The Mission and fall on its door with both my fists.

Footsteps immediately answer my call, just as my Foster Mother reaches me, grabbing my arm, and twisting me away. I pull out of her grip and turn to find Sister standing before us. She glances over her shoulder, towards the voice of The Missionary, which is insistent, soothing, as he speaks to someone deep within the shadows. Sister steps out into the light and crosses her pale hands over the dark skirt of her cloth. Her fingers are long and thin, the nails like shells, see-through, lilac pink, with a half-moon inside each one. She studies me also, from my feet, which are bare, to my large brown hands, which clutch my *pareu* against my belly, to my face, which does not seem to please her.

Foster Mother lets go of my arm and makes the sign of the God our Son over her chest then speaks the words of our greeting.

Ia Ora Na.

You have returned already?

She was just visiting, Sister.

Good, because it has been settled, I believe.

She wants to thank you for blessing her marriage.

He likes you very much, doesn't he?

What has been settled?

Besotted is the word, won't have any other.

We must go now, daughter.

I had hoped you would not become another island trollop.

She must not miss her coach.

But we are powerless when it comes to the desire of men.

Thank you, Sister.

What has been settled?

Remember Teha'amana, the stories in The Gospel are not myth, and Noah's Ark was as big as this island, our home.

The women pronounce the day. They kneel before the king and reveal themselves, their breasts, while I edge my feet in the water, curled up. I gaze into your river of yellow, and green, blue and orange, and red.

When I was beginning, just growing, before I was thrust out into the light, the women carried shrimp, tender crab, and *tunny* fish in their *umete*, balancing the long wooden plates on their heads, between their hands, humming like the birds, because the words of their songs were *tapu*.

I was not born on the day they pulled Oro down from the *marae*, the day the wooden shell of Ta'aroa was given to the first white ones, the day the king ate turtle before offering it to the gods, the day the women sat down and ate beside their men. No, I was not born on that day, the day the king did not die, and my people were not struck down as they slept.

Though, I like to think it was that day, hallowed, a beginning, but I was still dreaming, curled up by your river, my toes in the water, waiting.

I was born under a single steady flame. Foster Mother named me for strength. I suckled her from night through to first light, while the women collected their tears in their hands, just as the earth possesses the rain. And they remembered all the sacred images, the women, once wrapped in red feathers, bound with sennit, and soaked in fragrant oil. And they thought of their gods being pulled down, of their ancestors being defeated. Of the stories that lived deep within, which would have to be cut out with a long knife.

And their bodies ached, not with bringing children into the world, but with knowing everything from before.

I stay here, at the edge, my feet in the water, waiting, the waves breaking, somewhere far off. You call this one, Day of the God.

Hina was the daughter of Kui the blind and they lived together, these two, on the cliff tops in the south most eastern tip of the island of Mangaia. One of these cliffs had a cave with an opening that faced the sea and a rock pool lay at its feet, where Hina would go down to bathe.

The water from Kui's taro fields, when it overflowed, ran all the way to the entrance of the cave, and out the other side, into the pool, the lagoon beyond, and the ocean further still. In Hina's pool lived a great number of eels and they were her friends, winding their way round her legs as she bathed. She was not afraid.

One day, Hina noticed an eel more magnificent than the rest and this eel of eels dared to touch her in the place between her legs, and because she liked it, she let it come again. This eel gave Hina so much pleasure she hurried to the rock pool as soon as her father left for his taro fields.

She would throw down her pareu and walk into the pool, naked, and shameless, and wanting.

One morning, while Hina was waiting, daydreaming, this mischievous eel wove its way through her reflection, and changing shape, rose up before her in the form of a man, tall as a tree, with skin burnished brown. He told her, I am Te Tuna, god of eels. Will you lie down with me?

And she did, Hina, without a moment's hesitation, so bold was she. They made love right there on the rocks, with the white terns watching, and the clouds, and the waves, which threw themselves up against the island's ancient reef.

Afterwards, each day, Hina came in secret, to meet her man, her god, and they made love on the rocks beside the pool, while her father toiled beneath the sun, harvesting taro for their evening meal. And they also went, these two, in secret, to the home of Kui, and slept together on her father's bed, no words passing between their lips. Until one day, Te Tuna spoke for a second time, and he told Hina this:

Tomorrow, there will be a terrible storm, the rain will not stop falling, will fall for days on end and many lives will be lost. The water will drown out your father's fields, and when it does I'll swim here and lay my head on your windowsill. When my head is on your paepae, you must take the adze of your ancestors, hanging there on the hook beside the doorway.

She listened, Hina, with fathomless eyes, and did not utter one word of protest, Hina-moe-aitu, who slept with a god.

That night, the rain began to fall on her father's leaf roof. There was thunder in the sky like the world splitting in two, and lightening turned the black sky purple. The rain fell, without pause, without breath, and it did not cease even when the morning light crept like a spider through darkened skies. Kui the blind lay fearfully beside his daughter, and clung to her, not a wink had he slept all night.

The water had risen so high it now covered the head of his taro plants and soon it reached their door.

Then, as he had promised, the great eel came, and placed his head on the windowsill. Hina, seeing him, spoke gently to her father, she said, don't worry, Papi, stay here on our bed, don't move. Kui could not see his daughter climb down from their bed, could not see her wade through the water, he did not see her clasp the adze of his tupuna, and chop off the great eel's head with one fell swoop.

The rain immediately stopped, and the sun came out to dry up the land. Great pools of water, which had run into rivers, into themselves, quickly evaporated.

Hina took Te Tuna's head to the burying place behind her house, and each day, she paid a visit to her lover's grave. Ten nights went by before a bright green shoot pushed up through the earth. It wasn't like anything she'd ever seen before, and she watched it with a fierce devotion, until it grew tall and strong. It climbed up towards the clouds, and in time, her sons scaled it, to twist free the precious green fruit that hung in abundance from its branches.

It was the very first coconut tree on the island. There was sweet nourishing water to drink from the green nuts, soft pulpy flesh on the inside, which became hard and white, and creamy milk was squeezed from it. From the dried flesh, baked by the sun, there was oil, which the women scented with blossom, and rubbed into their skin, their scalps.

The leaves were used for baskets, for shade, for the roofs of dwelling houses, from the shells, bowls were fashioned, the husks, their fiber was twisted to make rope, and finally the old tree, once dying, was cut down, its body used for the pillars in communal huts. All was used, and cherished. Is used and cherished, throughout the land.

When the husk is pulled away from the outer shell, Te Tuna's face can be seen once more, the god of eels, who swam in Hina's water of life, with his two round eyes and surprised mouth.

Te Tuna gave us a gift, Hina told her children, and her children told it to theirs, and it is told, still, to this day.

I watch from behind the mango tree, its dark trunk hiding me, watch you squatting by the doorway, in the same position as the day I left. That will be your third cigarette since waking, and your second, of tea, which will be laced with absinthe, unless the bottle stands empty.

Your face seems older in just two days, the skin so pale the green of the mountain is reflected in it. Your eyes are black beads that move over the valley, and up to the sky, then down towards the women who sit outside your landlord's house on the verandah.

I move forward as quietly as my bare feet will carry me. When the women stop their sewing, their whispering, and their laughing, when they hear the rustle of my foot on a dry leaf, they turn to greet me with tight-lipped smiles. It is only then, you see me. You rise quickly, and put out your cigarette before it is finished, and as I walk past you to enter inside, you softly spit out these words:

I thought the bird had flown?

The same human beings inhabit your walls. They sit, they lie, they stand, they dance, they sigh, and they keep quiet. They keep the word of god inside their breasts, just as their temples keep the cross. You will poke, prod, nudge, tease, and I am already in Hell, because that is what it must be, without the fire. I'd like to close my eyes, but you will tell me to open them. Open your eyes, you will say, I've spent too many years with my eyes closed!

Did you close them once, when you lay down beside your true wife, a woman who looks as though happiness left her a long time ago? The woman you keep hidden in your wooden box, leaving the key for me to find beside the breadcrumbs and the empty tins. She waits patiently with your children, all of them dressed in black apart from the girl. Every day, they wait in a room with sunlight pouring over their sad faces. Your true wife looks like the sturdy trunk of a tree and your children the branches coming out of her.

In the beginning, when you loved her, I imagine your skin must have been smooth and taut as a green mango. And I imagine you kissed her eyes shut.

You take my parcel from me but don't untie the knot. You don't lay the food out, or my mother's cloth where it now belongs. You just say, let's go to bed. She still watches from her place above the doorframe, Olympia. They all watch, but pretend not to, their eyes following us, they listen from beyond the wall, ears twitching, and I want to be quiet, so quiet, but you don't allow it.

I fix my gaze sideways, just above your head, to the right, and put myself in that cold bright world high up on the hill. I can hear the cry of the black birds soaring across the valley, the flapping of their wings, and the crackling of the flames beneath the tired faces of the women, their wide hips concealed under layers of cloth. The dogs are thirsty, and want to stop, take rest, but must carry on, follow the master.

I can smell the dark scent of their fur, as you grab the skirt of my dress and pull it up to my waist, and over my limbs, so that I'm naked again, before you, man who makes human beings.

All the blood rushes to your face now, colours it aflame, and it looks like you will burst. The veins protrude on your brow, your temples – the temple where I kneel, where I pray, where I must place a kiss. Kiss, you say, kiss me. At last, you say, at last. A dog growls beyond the bamboo reeds, on the other side of the road, at the foot of our bed. The sea rises, and falls back, tumbling, it sighs, repeating the same words, at last, at last. The dog growls again, but I can't see it. It rises up on its hind legs like a human being to take my island in its arms, to carry it, protect it, the fear rising inside its chest to become a deep whimpering cry.

They stand on the road that takes them from Faaone to Taravao, watching the waves break. The white of the surf encircles the island, at every moment, hour, and colour of the day. The ancient wall holds back the ocean. The *makatea* protects, and carries upon it, within it, the stories of the archipelagos, its gods, and goddesses, its human beings who possess a past of unspeakable wonder.

Foster Mother releases her girl's hand and tells her to try, try again. She reminds her that he is a good man. That she must be patient, and it will get better, that love will grow. Love, she says, will sow itself here. And she presses the palm of her hand to her daughter's navel. Teha'amana grips her true mother's hand in her own, and moves it to the place where the heart lives, where it clamours and asks to be listened to. Foster mother obeys. Then, she releases her mother's hand from her body and turning away, walks on without a backward glance.

Finally, The Painter comes. Foster Mother's parcel sits in the middle of the dirt floor, dark blue and bright yellow, unopened.

He falls on her, a dead weight, gasping for breath, released from the anxiety, the anger, the uncertainty.

He falls on her, where they lie, on this bed, his bed, a proper bed, at least, she had thought.

She thinks. But he does not crush her, Teha'amana, because she was named for strength.

A storm swept in from the sea and lightning struck a *tamanu* tree in half on *marae taputapuatea*. The severed part fell into the water and floated on the surface, without sinking, until it was borne away by the tide, between the waves.

It was our ancestors who witnessed the event on the island of Oro's birth. Sacred Raiatea!

The high priest stood at the altar, unable to spell out its meaning, but that night, his dreams came to him, clear and fast. He saw a boat without an outrigger, cutting through dark water, bringing with it a new race, their weapons more powerful than our own. When the cockerel announced the day, the priest rose quickly and went to inform the king of his dream. He predicted the coming of strangers from across the circle of the sea.

Our many traditions will be lost, he said, including the beating of *tapa*, and we will allow it, allow ourselves to be cut in two.

I imagine all the girls before me, and the fathers who rowed their daughters out to meet the first ships, and the strangers, who were like magicians. They gave us gifts from hidden compartments in their clothes, their cloth, which was softer than *tapa*.

A girl for a nail, a red feather, a shiny button, anything. Everything was new, sacred. Superior.

But they were not fragrant, these men, they were sick, their teeth stained and rotten. So we healed them with fruit from the land, bathed them in crystal clear pools, and rubbed their skin with *monoi*, 'til they gleamed. We welcomed their blood, to mix with our own.

And we let them possess us, the women, possess our bodies, our voices. Because we believed then we would possess them too.

You have pulled my *pareu* away, so you can see, all of me. That is how I like it, how it should be, once was, you say. I keep my eyes closed. Pretend I'm still asleep. I am lying on my front, the left side of my face pressed to your pillow, turned to the doorway, as always.

Your hands hover just above, I imagine, where my shoulder blades meet. You would like to bring them down, to touch, stroke, rub, but you don't. Not now, you say, not now, a whisper. But they can hear, the ones who watch.

Your stool creaks. The water laps over the edge of the little gourd as you bend down to place it by your feet, just as the river sometimes breaks its banks. Your instruments scrape against paper as you work quickly. You don't wake me, and I don't know how long I can pretend, before you know. But I think you already know, so that we are both pretending...

The *torome* hops on his long thin legs and searches the river bank for something to eat, anything that moves. His eyes are the darkest brown, with a splash of white above each one, as though you have put them there with your brush. His belly is dark red, darker than blood, the colour that blood becomes when it dries. His back is black-feathered, and his wings too, the tips of them the colour of his eyes, which are deep brown, and that red, of dried blood. He wants to take flight, the *torome*, and begins to make short, shallow flapping sounds, before lifting off, and gliding towards the lagoon, which today is not clear. A thick mist hangs above the mountain wall, obscuring each peak. No, today is not his lucky day.

But the *torome* does not exist. He lives in my mind, to pass the time, as you make me. He was the very last of his kind, and lived alone, fearful, and fearless, unaware of his beauty. The last time he was seen was a hundred years before I was born, beside a stream. A white man who travelled here on the ship of Cook saw him, and made a picture.

I crept forward, to get a better look, but it flew away, the Tahitian Sandpiper, this rare creature, the white man said.

I want to get up now. Want to pick my dress up from where it fell, to pull it over me, to cover myself. But I know not to. I cannot, must not, because you are making me, and I must have your permission first. To rise, to move even a finger, to uncross my ankles, straighten my arm, to arch my neck so it creaks like the hollow trunk of a bamboo reed, to wash the sleep from my eyes.

You will tell me not to move, to stay like that, and keep on looking at you. You will ask me what I am thinking. You will snort like a pig, when I reply, nothing. Nothing, you will repeat. Yes, you will say, it is better that way. I'll put some thoughts in your head. And this is the story you will tell.

That you came home late one night, having missed the coach, or it having broken down between Papeete and Mataiea, and when you got back, everything was bathed in darkness. I was lying naked on your bed, my body shaking with fear, because I thought you were a ghost, because I carry this belief, which is buried deep, which even The Missionary cannot pluck out. And you ask me tell it to you again, this belief, in the same way I used to ask my Foster Mother for a story that belongs to the ancient wall, the *makatea* of our island. And to urge me, you coax, by tracing a finger from my tailbone to the nape of my neck, and you place a kiss behind my right ear, against my skull bone. I'll create a story around this picture to whet their appetites, you will say, you said, and you say it again.

Save me! Save me! It is evening, the evening of the gods. Watch over me, close to me, my dear Lord.

Protect me from enchantments, and from sudden death. Protect me from bad deeds, useless gossip, and the anger of others.

Protect from intrigue, and from quarrels concerning property and land. Protect me, from the fury of the clan.

Protect me, dear God, from the one who takes pleasure in making me tremble, and keep my soul safe until morning light, O Lord.

Prayer finished, Foster Mother opens her eyes, focusing slowly on her hands, which are half shadows in her lap. She flicks a look at the shelf, which is almost empty, just a few tins remaining. She has not enjoyed the white man's food. She fixes her gaze now on the inside of her *pandanu* leaf roof.

She looks and carries on looking, her mind drifting, eyes widening like a night creature's, to compensate for the lack of light. She can see all of it as though in a dream, but knows it is a nightmare, the face of the child before the girl, the forehead bloodied, the eyelids unmoving, the lips turned blue. They placed him, the boy, in her trembling arms, perfectly intact, his hands clenched into fists, which would not open, though she tried her best to pry them apart. He had to restrain her, her *tane*. She can still see the face of her man when he refused to meet her look. And she already knew what he was thinking, that this woman, his *vahine*, would never give, that her womb was a graveyard, and what he would do in time.

The tears have all dried up now, like an empty riverbed before the rains. Except, there will be no rain, sun, nor lightening, no breezes from the South and the East, to join together, to make her yield. But why think of those things now? She lies down, turning onto her side, squeezing her eyes shut to banish the memory once more. Why think of those things now, she repeats the question to herself, filling her lungs fully, opening her eyes suddenly, as though the answer sits waiting before her. Exhaling slowly, she stares at the empty mat beside the doorway. If only he had opened his eyes for a moment, a breath.

And that is her final thought before she is plucked from reality to the land of *Po*, The Good Book in one hand, and the past in the other.

She was not my Eve, no, she was not that, but my wife, is still, strong-willed, powerful, and wise. She was good in bed too. We had an idyllic honeymoon as I recall. Didn't leave our rented rooms for a week, though we spent one sublime afternoon traipsing the Louvre, rubbing up against one another like dogs in heat, where I fell in love all over again, but this time with Delacroix.

The children came, one after the other, each and every year, a blessing, five blessings, and at night, between the freezing cold and the warmth of the stove, we discussed everything from Romanticism to Impressionism, and the Theory of Evolution. We agreed, resolutely, all the stories in the Bible were myth, and I believed us equals, that she understood me, and I her, but without warning, she took them away, the fruit of my loins, to this place, her home, her hearth, "where we shall be secure", she said.

I tried to do my best, to do my duty, be a good husband, but I am not. I cannot sacrifice.

The girl is the spit of my mother, and appears each night, like a faithful dog, to be near me, her father whom she loves, and for this I am grateful. Yet, it fills me with a deep regret.

My heart aches to see her press away copious tears, fingertips blue with cold. I would tell her this, if I only could. Be a girl, wear dresses, go dancing, fall in love, and if your suitors ask who your father is, tell them with pride, tell them, each one, what he does, where he has gone, and why.

I would give her the necklace of coral I bought in Papeete on the day of my departure. I would pin it around her swan-like neck when she has on her first ball gown, and I would tell her – how pretty mademoiselle looks, how savage, a girl wearing coral instead of pearls!

The colour reminded me of the soles of your feet when I held them in the palms of my hands, once, a long time ago. Though it feels like only yesterday.

You opened your eyes, which were brown, flecked with gold, and laid claim to my heart. How you transformed it.

But a whole world separates us now, and she will never know, never learn of my intention.

And I would like to tell it to you, my Teha'amana, as you lie here beside me, only a whisper away, about the time before, when my wife was far. I was alone, and lonely, completely wretched. I lived in a room beneath the pavements with one window framed by bars, where fallen leaves scratched up against the glass. I paid for love – that was my food – it was better than coal for the stove, or steak tartare.

When I set sail for Tahiti, I heard she was dying, the one I'd loved amongst many.

Do you understand what I'm trying to say? I want to tell it to you now, because we are safe, hidden away here in this attic, in the city of the merchants' harbor. But listen, the rain, it falls once more.

Once, it fell above us, wildly, like clattering hooves on the leaf roof, on the skin of the river, and the still lagoon, through the night it fell, invading every corner of the island. But here it strums meekly against the pane, politely on roofs of slate, filling the gutters until they run over.

Then the water falls across the cobblestones, and in between the gravestones, where I cannot walk barefoot. Or I would catch my death.

The shadow crouches at the foot of our bed, where you have put it, just out of reach, out of sight. It never reveals its true face, but watches and waits with more patience than a tree bound to this round earth.

Sometimes a hand creeps over to caress the heel of my foot, but one small kick from me, sends it away, back where it belongs, to the edge of the bed. You have put this thing, this being, man, woman, or child, placed it inside, beside me, forever. It speaks between the light and the surface of your painting.

He was a boy, a beautiful one at that, with hair the colour of fire, of sun-ripened oranges, which fell in waves to frame the face of an angel. His eyes were as pure as the light that fell on the Aegean Sea. From an early age, one glance from him, and girls, women, and men alike would be struck dumb, bathing in the afterglow of his pernicious smile. Which was a rare thing, because for the most part, he was a spoilt-brat who ignored the existence of other people.

Why was he this way? Those in the village blamed the mother. She forgave his sins, turned a blind eye to her pride and joy. He could do no wrong, because he was hers, and she comforted herself with the fact he was young "and I must not clip his wings". At home, he ruled the roost, throwing himself up against the furniture and screaming at the top of his lungs while she carried on sewing, stirring the stew, the apple pie. At fourteen, with sheepdog and some routine imposed, he herded the lambs, the rams and ewes across the hills, to and from his mother's smallholding. He spent long hours idling, sprawled beneath his favorite tree, an ancient cedar, which he was also fond of climbing.

One day, a huge fox with red claws appeared. With stout black legs it approached the herd, its dark pelt struck through with flashes of orange and white. Instead of allowing his sheepdog to challenge this imposing creature, he held it back by the scruff, watching with fear and excitement as the fox picked out a helpless lamb, and dragged it away, bleating, by its neck. It thrilled him and he kicked his poor dog away in irritation, so heartless was he.

Later that evening, he told his mother the reason for the loss to their herd. He had fallen asleep and their useless sheepdog had run off to play. Of course, she believed him and punished the dumb creature by beating it and starving it that night. The next day, the boy found an old man asleep beneath his favorite tree and he angrily picked up a stone and threw it at him. It hit the side of his face and the man awoke with a cry, frightening the birds from the trees and causing the clouds to cover the sun.

The old man searched the face before him for a hint of remorse, but the boy merely laughed, though his heart skipped a beat by the directness of the stranger's gaze.

The old man cupped a hand to his wound and stood full height. He was taller than the ancient cedar and his white hair, which now fell to the ground, twisted and danced around his form like terrible snakes.

I am Apollo, he said, and because of your wickedness, you will be cursed and that curse will destroy and devour your physical beauty and spiritual soul. Pustules will ooze from that face of yours and your limbs, and you will be driven to hide yourself at all costs because one look at you will make men scream in horror.

Then, Apollo ascended to the skies, gave the command, open, and the heavens obliged. The sheep cowered in a huddle and the boy's faithful dog now really did run off, never to be seen again. The boy knelt down beside the foot of the cedar and hid his young face with shivering hands.

He stayed in that position until the clouds uncovered the moon, and his mother's voice could be heard from afar, calling his name across the hills, over and over.

Syphilis!

Syphilis!

He makes me from the trunk of the *pua keni keni*, gives me a mouth swollen with anger, eyes the shape of leaves, and colours them black.

The story goes like this. He cut me down in the interior, went there with a boy, a young man, the woodcutter named Jotefa who promised to show him a place where the *pua* trees grew, have been growing for a thousand years, untouched, deep in the valley. He went there gladly, and walking behind this Jotefa, had a feeling, a desire to kill, to fuck that boy he imagined a girl. He cut me down until his hands bled.

He cried out at the end of his endeavour, while the forest also resounded with his cries, with these three words. I am savage.

He captures it in his diary, his journey to the interior, lest he should forget the details of that day, and his metamorphosis.

He makes a hollow in the back of my head and carves another Eve there, reaching for the lower branches, so she will always be, about to pluck, to commit, and be driven away from the first home, the garden inside my skull. He calls me The Head of a Tahitian Woman but I am the reflection of her face in wood, the one who comes close when he has gone out for his morning walk. She traces the bridge of my nose, my wide nostrils, my thick lips, my short brow, and my jutting-out chin.

It is as though she is looking at herself for the first time, with someone else's hand.

When he returns, she asks him why he has given her black leaves for eyes, but he merely replies, it is finished.

And he places me on the shelf, between the empty tins of corned beef and the condensed milk, below the absinthe, and above the crumbs of stale bread. My *pua* wood face listens, because it is all I can do.

He wakes, and his movements wake her too, but she does not stir, the flutter of the eyelids would give her away, but he does not see. She keeps her body completely still, like the pictures on his walls, like the key sitting in the lock of his wooden chest, like the family trapped behind glass, between a frame, a family who will never see the light of a Tahitian day.

Sweat drips from every pore of his ragged body. It begins at the crown of his head, clumping the hair together like seaweed, and drips down his skull, behind the ears, the back of the neck, and along the length of the spine. Sweat covers his entire torso, collects at the crease of each limb. He peels himself from the sheets, which are stained with his dread.

In the middle of the hut, he strikes a lonely figure, as though stranded on a boat, lost in an ocean of dark, a dark grotto, where he surrenders. He holds out his arms, suspending them above his head, crossing the palms one over the other.

He has been crucified and resurrected, time and time again, in the minds of men.

He lets his arms fall, defeated, and turns away, emitting a long and painful sigh. He walks naked towards the open doorway, the sky, a pale yellow in the beckoning dawn. She peels one eye open to know what he is doing then closes it quickly, relieved, hoping he'll not return to bed. She reaches out behind her to feel the soaking wet sheet, hand recoiling in horror.

The image of him is burned within, squatting beside their oil lamp. On the diadem, between Orohena and Arorai, where the spirits roam free, the flame cannot protect, does not, will not protect. She recites the prayer she was taught as a child, which straddles both worlds. At dusk they say it, in that elusive hour, when everything is covered in a glaze of gold.

He squats before the doorway, staring into the flame of the oil lamp, trying to remember, to recall the dream in the darkness behind his eyes.

The images begin to unfold. He stands at the edge of a grotto, on its banks, and places a hand on a mossy stone. The door opens, and he enters, steps inside a cave, a vault of ancient oaks, and murmuring cedars. Guided by a familiar voice, he follows a path beside rivers of lapis-blue, which flow out from this subterranean landscape to a distant ocean. He walks along cliff tops that fall away into chasms, deep and yawning.

It feels as though he has been walking forever when it was only moments ago he was listening to the gurgling of the river, to the clatter of horse hooves on gravel, and to the call of the cuckoo in the forest.

Now he is here, has arrived at the chamber situated at the very core of the earth. All around him, the women in his paintings are at work, his Eves, plucked from Paradise, they reside here, all forms of her, the one that lies naked on his bed. They are hard at work, chiseling away at the rock, sifting the rubble, melting and tempering the substance men think so precious, the cure to the sickness that ravages the world, old and new, that which they call Mercury.

The voice hangs like a garland around his neck, a sash around his middle, the sweetest bouquet. The voice does not belong to one of his Tahitian Eves but to his beloved mother, his first True Eve. She appears before him with dark doe eyes, carrying a bowl of that prized liquid silver and without a word, pours it over her son's afflicted body, repeating the action thrice.

It burns, dissolves, and heals the incurable disease, obliterates the ulcers that decorate his skin, his groin, his limbs, and his face, which has become a mask of horror. He falls to his knees, holding his hands out before him then turns them over like the pages of a book, his book.

Slowly, deliberately, he traces his own mouth, the nose, the hollows of his face, as though for the first time.

They are smooth once again. He looks up at her, his beautiful mother, with wonder and gratitude, his heart crushed with sorrow, and he addresses the ghost-goddess towering before him.

All I can remember is a dark room and being cradled into it, in the arms of a stranger. You were lying on a bed. It was like you were sleeping. I didn't want to be there, but outside, climbing the guava trees beneath the blazing Peruvian sun. Now I dream always of returning to that moment, which is lost, which is myth, forever committed to memory.

I would take hold of your hand, and look into your face, and stay with you until they put you in the ground.

Go now, my son, you must return to the bright light of day, and finish your good work, the world is waiting for it.

I was angry with you for leaving me.

I know, but it was not my choice, it was God's.

And with that, she pulls him up onto his feet and turns him around, pressing the tips of her fingers into the small of his back, giving him a gentle nudge. He takes a few reluctant steps. Does not want to be parted from her again, but obeys, and moves forward with resignation. When he glances behind him, she is gone.

What is she holding, the girl on the bench?

A note from the doctor to say she is clean.

Clean from what?

The British Disease...

How do you know?

Do you walk around with your ears and your eyes closed?

Do they all carry notes?

Some do not.

And what do they say if the men ask?

They will shrug their shoulders and promise they are well.

And the men believe them?

Yes, the ones who are desperate, just off the ships, or the ones who are sick themselves.

How does the sickness arrive?

Like the first boat without an outrigger, suddenly.

Dear Diary,

Another letter has arrived and this time, to my complete surprise and utter delight, Maman handed it over to me, unopened. She has instructed me to hide all correspondence from Papa in my room and not to speak a word of it to Mormor. I am allowed to read it first then give her a short summary after she has had her afternoon nap. I heard her footsteps on the stair, the key turning in the lock, and her brocade curtains being drawn to keep out the light.

I am now in sole possession of any future news. I will keep Papa's letters between the pages of this diary, at the bottom of my trunk. Maman believes Mormor has been rifling through her possessions, trying to find details of any secret plans Papa might be drawing us into.

Papa has begun a new painting with the same girl as the central figure. He has put her in a blue and white striped "Missionary Dress", which they all wear since their conversion to Christianity some fifty years ago. That means she never knew anything different. Strange to think of her reciting The Lord's Prayer. The dress belongs to an old native woman, and was traded in for Papa's lucky waistcoat, which this woman greatly admired. He has allowed himself to be parted from his favorite piece of clothing! I have never seen him not wearing it. When I think of Papa, I see him in his embroidered waistcoat, and I can still remember reaching out to count the number of triangles, blue and green, that sat within bands of orange and scarlet, the colours faded, and some of its threads coming undone.

This woman who now owns a piece of my childhood was once the member of a fearsome cult that practiced infanticide for the love of a pagan god who went by the name of Oro. The women of this religious order called themselves the *Areois*, and made a pledge upon entering that they would live for freedom of the flesh (sex!) and not procreation. They avoided motherhood at all costs but if it did transpire (getting pregnant), then those born to them would be suffocated at birth by their own hand. All except their first-born were destined to suffer this fate, and that is how in turn they controlled the numbers of their kind.

Papa was introduced to this elderly native at a wedding reception for two young Tahitians, Christian converts, which they have all become. The bride's belly was already quite swollen with child, The Missionary seemingly turning a blind eye to the fact, which made Papa rather suspicious. Suspicious of what, he did not say.

The old woman had an indecipherable symbol stamped upon her left cheek by the French authorities, as a stark reminder to the rest of the population of the sins of their past. And yet, they themselves have banned the tradition of this permanent inking method called tattoo, which originates from the Tahitian word *tatau*. They have succeeded in driving into the mountains the natives who still practice this art form, if one can call it that.

Papa thinks it a stroke of genius to put the girl in the dress of the old woman, and he will call this new painting Teha'amana has many Ancestors. She will be holding a traditional fan made of *pandanu* leaves (a tree native to the region) and he will place behind her right shoulder, the spectre of their goddess Hina, once worshipped with an equal reverence to their god Oro. Papa says the story of Hina is not known as one definitive myth.

In each island of Oceania, they tell their own version of her story, so that she possesses many truths and exists in numerous different forms.

That must be her name then, the girl, his muse: Teha'amana. I wonder what she thought when he asked her to put on the dress? Did she oblige willingly? Did Papa have to bribe her, cajole her?

Now, I understand why The Missionaries felt it their duty to civilise the heathens, to put an end to such barbaric practices. I wonder if she, Teha'amana, allows herself to think of what existed before, or if she is even aware of it? How would she feel about the unimaginable horror of what they did, the *Areois*? It is sure to give me nightmares.

No, I do not agree with Papa when he says the Church has destroyed everything noble and good in these people in order to impose on them a new belief-system...in the guise of Enlightenment. I would like to put this argument to him:

If they had been allowed to carry on as before without intervention, how many more babies would have died in the hands of their mothers? The fact remains. We are all God's Children, each one of us conceived by the miracle of The Creator, and we possess a higher conscience than that of animals. What God would ask such form of violent allegiance?

I told him, I am a Christian now, and I do not want to go back into the darkness. He seemed disappointed, wanted the dress off my back in exchange for a bottle of rum. I told him I preferred his waistcoat with its colourful threads. It is a little tight, I admit, but something different that draws attention in the village. I am a Christian now.

She was wearing a pink dress, faded and creased, hair unoiled, and carrying a look of insolence, his *vahine*. She pushed his hand away, when he offered her the gift of my dress. I do not blame her. What girl wants an old woman's cloth, and one who is marked?

He was watching her every move, even as he spoke to me, and to the others at our table, his eyes following her as she rose, without a word to him, to fill her plate for a third time, bold young thing, she did not care what people thought. He watched as she helped herself to another drink. You could see she had already had more than enough, the way she was swaying on her bare feet. My *vahine*, he said, smiling, through clenched teeth, I'll have to drag her fourteen-year-old backside home...God help me...but...I like them fat and vicious...intelligence is too spiritual for me. And he laughed loudly, but no one else joined, because we were unsure what he meant by those words. No, I don't want to go back into the darkness. There were always, in those days, many hours until night fell, when the hogs were wrapped in coconut leaves and hot stones placed over them, when the earth ovens were lit.

The sun went more slowly then. Goes slowly still, in good time, moving across the sky obediently, because of Maui.

He beat the sun into submission, a long time ago. O, yes, he did.

Your love is the colour of forest berries, rotting. Do you hear me, painter-man?

Once, I lived in a garden where the boldest and brightest flowers grew, where I watched the secret journey of the ants, the birds, the bees, the trees, and the stars. Now, I must suffer in the darkness, for your Art, with no choice but to listen to the voices, the lives opening and closing, like the doors in your world below.

I am bound to your true wife, we two, are leaves of a single stem, and the knowing settles behind my eyes, the lids of which are kept open by invisible twigs.

In the silence of this forever night, the whisper of tears carries up through the gaps of the dark wood floor.

In the silence of my open cage, I listen to the breath of death beside me, close to me, and I've grown used to the fingers that caress the soles of my upturned feet.

And the sound of this strange city seeps through me just as my island's existence did.

All the beauty I once knew lives only in the mind now, pieces of a broken dream. I summon them up, one by one, so they sing, sleep here, beside me, on this pillow, the river, the sea, the lizard, the leaves, the bamboo, the dogs, and the cockerels.

And you, your voice gurgled, and whispered, rustled, and yawned, creaked and sang. And you cried too.

The door opens and your girl enters inside, the light of her lamp flickering over her young face, which reminds me of a fresh, unopened flower. She's still a child, but pain has already made a home in her heart. Her breath catches as she kneels down before you. She kisses the tips of her fingers then brings them your closed mouth. She strokes the hair on your head, as though tidying it, like a mother would.

She turns to me, her gaze softening, eyes shining like just-lit flames. She places the palm of her right hand over the top of mine then takes it away, looking at me, questioningly.

She asks – I am sure your little finger was flush against your ring finger yesterday. Have you moved it, because it is now jutting out just so?

Her eyelid twitches while she waits for my answer, knowing there'll be none. She reaches out to touch my elbow, my shoulder, traces the curve of it then runs her index finger down my spine, as you used to, from the nape of my neck to my buttocks, then along the inside of my right thigh, to my calf, the heel, the arch of my foot.

She traces my little toe and the big toes of both my feet where they are stuck together.

She looks at her finger to see if my colour has come off then presses it to her lips, which are red as the inside of a pomegranate fruit. She closes her eyes, and a tear escapes from the deep pool that lies within. She rises suddenly, as though shaking herself free of the thought of me, snatching up her lamp, and hurrying from the room, this box, this dark, where I'm shut up.

He promises she can go to Church, as soon as the bell rings out. In the meantime, for the rest of the day, she must be good, must sit quietly, in the blue and white striped dress she does not want to wear. She glances up at her worn copy of The Gospel, where he has banished it, nestling between two empty bottles of absinthe.

She concedes, settling herself down on the stool, pulling at the cloth of her skirt, picking up the fan from the floor where she threw it, holding it over the heart where The Missionary told her feelings live. He, her *tane*, tells her she is grumpy today because she has a sore head. He had to drag her home last night, that she humiliated him; he felt like a fool in front of all those people.

She retorts – but you don't care what people think.

Rankled, he tells her to keep still and shut up, the words tumbling out of his mouth before he can stop them. She makes a loud squeaking sound, like a bird under attack, and flings her fan down again in anger. Bracing himself for yet another scene, he puts his brushes aside and comes to her, kneeling, in a practiced gesture. He begs her forgiveness, pressing the pads of his hands together, humbling himself before her. He tells her she is a goddess and must be worshipped as such, but she replies, refusing to meet his eyes: I am a girl, not a goddess! He sighs in agreement, yes, I am wrong. Trying to appease, to pacify this girl who is woman, also child. He picks up the fan, and gently pushes the handle back into her left fist.

Yes, you are a girl, and better than each and every one here, hanging on the walls of this palace. After the painting is finished, I will buy you cloth for a new dress. What is your favourite colour?

She rolls her eyes, indignantly. White, she whispers, and holds up her fan, with renewed reluctance. As he turns back towards the easel, he mumbles, white is not a colour.

She drops one curved edge of the fan against her right wrist. Eyes still flashing with anger, she pokes her tongue out at him, but he does not see.

The god of the ocean sleeps. In his room, he slumbers, beyond the reef. On the far side of the sea, across a dark expanse of water, in the deep, he sleeps.

Teahoroa and Ro'o spear a shrimp's head to their hook, which is made from whalebone, the line from olona fibre. They've gone out further than they should, than they usually dare, not realising this is the watery home of Ruahatu. Throwing their line far and wide, the hook catches in the sleeping god's hair. Praying for a huge tunny, the boys grasp the line with all their might, and they pull. They heave, and they pull, and they wake Ruahatu from his precious dream.

We must go quickly, Teahoroa tells Ro'o, trembling. Terrified.

Go back and warn them, ask them to climb into their canoes, and go to to'a marama, rock of the moon, and wait there until his anger subsides.

Branches crackle and break, and tear from the trunks of the trees as water envelops the land. Ruahatu's fury is embodied in one giant wave after another. The ocean consumes everything. Saltwater washes away the temples, their stones, and their people, the ones who refused to believe, who did want to follow Teahoroa and Ro'o, and their families. Ruahatu swallows them whole.

There are no worshipping places where prayers can be made, no more upu marae. All the birds take refuge in the clouds, because they are the ata of the gods, their shadows on earth. The sea covers sacred Raiatea, the slopes of Mount Temehani, and finally its peak, until nothing more can be seen.

Until Sea mirrors Sky, and they become lovers once more, Papa and Rangi. And everything returns to the beginning, in the great deluge.

He tugs at the skirt of her blue and white striped dress, and asks her to stand, to pull it up, the cloth, and to keep it hoisted so he can see, tells her he's been fantasizing about it all day, knowing she was naked down there, and only a few feet away. She watches him unbutton his trousers and pull out his thing.

She's never liked the look of it but she looks, carries on looking. He asks her to kiss it.

All she can think of is the bell. That it will be struck soon. It will ring, cry out, and call her away, before long, at the next moment. She places the palms of her hands on the dirt floor while he spreads his on her broad shoulders.

The sound of his heart fills and empties the silence, and she remembers a similar noise from when she was small. When she was four, or five, or six.

I would light the lamp, as my Foster Mother taught me, as soon as Darkness fell. Beyond the cloth covering the opening, which was wetted with water to keep the insides cool, through the gaps of our bamboo reed walls came the sound of distant drumming, voices humming. I lay beside my mother, and clung to her still, when I was four, or five, or six. She told me it was the men in the valley, in the mountain, who slept beneath open skies, who were keeping our stories alive. And I used to imagine that we were those men, lying together beyond the doorway, on the forest floor, as she told me a story, the story of once, long ago.

Open your eyes, he tells her.

He commands, he sighs, he pleads, whispers, cries. I want to see your face looking up at me, with your mouth around my cock.

The coral rustles. The branches crackle. The sea murmurs to'a marama.

Teahoroa, and Ro'o, and their families, mothers and fathers, uncles and aunts, cousins, brothers, sisters, each one falls down exhausted on the rock of the moon, and they huddle there together, shivering. They cannot begin to imagine what the next day will bring or what the morning light will reveal, or if the red star will possess the strength to row his boat back across the shore. And to give one another strength, and hope, they sing. They knock on the door of the house of their ancestors. Some sit with their backs pressed up against one another, some lie curled around each other, with the words of their song, offerings on the tomb of the great ocean beyond.

Ta'aroa slept with the goddess of without.

Of them were born the white clouds, black clouds and the rain.

Ta'aroa slept with the goddess of within.

Of them was born the first seed, all that grows on the surface of the earth, the mist on the mountains, he who calls himself Strong, and she who calls herself Beautiful.

Ta'aroa slept with the goddess Hina.

Of them were born the rainbow, the moonlight, the red clouds and red rain.

Ta'aroa slept with the goddess of the bosom of the earth.

And of them was born Tefatou, the spirit who manifests himself in subterranean noises.

They carry their song through the night, on their tongues and in their bones, and they sleep a fitful sleep, until darkness is chased away by the first rays of the morning light, by the call of one of the banished birds, perched on a long white cloud. It is the voice of the sea swallow, the ata of Tane, one of Ta'aroa's offspring.

I look out to see parts of my island submerged, like my thoughts, like the past, and the memory of you.

What comes up now is the terrible thing you did. What you did when I asked you not to, when I told you, no. I said, stop.

But you did not listen. You were submerged in your green poison and could not taste my fear, could not feel my flesh, which had turned to iron, to wood, resisting every inch of you.

You came then. Then you cried, you shivered, and you shook inside.

You said – every nerve in my body, to the ends of each fibre of my being, even my teeth are shaking.

I felt then as the earth must feel the river beneath it, as the water flows through the rocks, across the stones, deep, deep under the ground.

I could hear the leaves trembling beyond the doorway, and the birds moving from branch to branch, speaking the words of their mysterious song,

"What is their god, if he has no mother or father and no wife, but a son."

Ro'o is the first one to notice the floodwaters recede. He hears the rustling of the coral and the whispering of the reef as they appear once more, and land, visible beneath the surface of the water. Listen, he tells his family, listen, look, look there.

Their island could be seen, clothed in shells, branches, broken twigs, and stones, and the bloated bodies of animals and human beings.

There is much work to do, clearing, and burying and building. So they climb back into their canoes, each one, to start the long journey home. All the birds follow them. They come down from the sky, the cockerel, the yellow thrush, the woodpecker, the whistling plover, the black parakeet, and the reef egret. They drop down from the clouds.

The spiders creep out from their hiding places. They spin bold, new webs in freshly built huts, and in between the branches of the trees, beside the river, in the caves high up on the plateaus.

The dragonfly returns, the ata of Hiro, god of thieves. The dead are buried and the babies are born.

Ro'o and Teahoroa and their clan are the ones who survive the great deluge. At first, they have only red clay and fish to eat. There is nothing to pick, or pluck from the land. But after two full moons, the green shoots of vegetation begin to appear and soon, there is uru, and taro, and fei to fill their bellies, and later, coconut to harvest. Soon, there is plenty, and the sleeping god is appeased.

He took things from all the islands.

Took the stone statues from Rapa Nui, to the west of Tahiti, stole them, or the image of them, and put their immense towering form on the crest of a hill, colouring the grass a yellow with quick brushstrokes. This painting would not have a woman in it, her body, would not contain her.

He took earplugs carved from *toromiro* wood the women once wore, to the east of Tahiti. In Rarotonga, they worshipped Tane, his death mask decorating their ears. And he placed these pieces of inspiration, like offerings along an imaginary fence bordering the hill, one steeped in a myth of his own making. In *Parahi Te Marae*, a plume of smoke rises up into a sky the colour of cornflowers, weeds like jewels in the cornfields of his youth.

She plunged into the river to wash his words away, and the taste of him.

He told her, your people come from Peru, did you know? Your people came from Peru thousands of years ago. They were the very first explorers, even before the Spanish, the French and the British. They travelled across the water in wooden rafts, following the stars and the movement of the waves, and made this island, this rock in the ocean, their own.

She asks him, what is Peru?

He tells her it is not an island, but a great, huge piece of land, to the east of Rapa Nui, which we now call Easter Island, the home of a fierce and noble race, the Incas.

She would like to ask why we call it Easter Island now, Rapa Nui. But she does not.

They worshipped the sun, the Incas, and the moon. They built temples to their gods and made sacrifices to them. Yes, they sacrificed children too!

She does not look into his eyes, which wait, but his hands, the nails, which she once thought were dug deep with dirt, except now she knows it is colour. She summons the words in her head, but they lie upon her tongue, stuck there, and she cannot bring herself to ask him that one question.

What did they do?

The sun and the moon, she thinks, the moon and the sun.

And her mind drifts to the image of the white tern, which lost all its feathers in flight when it flew from the moon to this island, hers, from night to day. The sun burned its wings and it fell, the white tern, into the black sand, exhausted, naked, with a branch from the *miro* tree clasped in its long ebony beak.

And that is why it is sacred, the *miro*, why it borders each temple that once stood, a symbol of terror in people's hearts, where they sacrificed children too.

She carries on looking at his hands, those worn fingers, which have made her, which keep on making, and she does not speak of it, the journey of the white tern, because it is a story, just one of the many that belong to her, and are hers alone.

The priestess brings me from my village because I am living in the shadow of our blessed mountain. She tells Mama she likes to have me because I am clean, my body strong, my face unmarked. Just blooming, she says, stroking my cheeks, tickling under my chin, making me laugh. And skin the colour of pure gold, she tells Mama.

She tells her I am the chosen, by Inti himself, and waits for Mama to speak but she does not. So I take the hand of the priestess, who promises I will live like a queen, and every day I will eat meat and maize.

I will miss Mama, but the priestess has skin soft as goat fur and eyes that crease and twinkle when she smiles. She gives me slippers made of pigskin, so I never have to walk barefoot again, and places on my head, a crown of sacred white feathers, but first she braids my hair, lovingly, into ten hundred plaits. Then she places coca leaves on my tongue and tells me to chew. Chew, she commands, chew. Then she says it softly when I begin to cry, promising me I will like it soon, and I chew harder, though it is bitter, just to please her.

I go home, back to my hut, in my sleep, past the branches of the lime trees, and when I reach there, Mama is waiting with her basket filled to the brim with potatoes dug up from the earth outside our hut. We wash and peel them as we used to, then boil and eat them, and they taste good, better than how I remember. I don't tell her I drink wine the colour of precious stone, instead of water from the mountain river. She asks if I am happy.

One day, the priestess wakes me, tells me I am fifteen and ready, and Inti waits.

She stands, her back pressed up against the wall as the men enter the temple to lead me out into the open with hot, wide hands.

The priestess does not answer when I ask for Mama, and she looks at me as though I am a stranger.

One of the men tells me it will be soon, and takes me in his arms like a straw doll when I say I cannot walk anymore. If I am fifteen, then I have not seen Mama for two years and she said she would come but she did not. If Inti's blood runs through me, then his blood runs through her, does it not?

The men give me more wine to drink so it warms my feet, my hands, but not the tip of my nose or my lips, which have gone numb with cold. They keep on telling me, it is not far, not long now, and their feet sink into the snow as we climb higher, keep on climbing. Forever, it seems.

I keep my eyes open, though they tell me to close them, and they give me more wine, pushing coca between my teeth.

Soon I am making my way through the lime trees again, the sun beating down on my back, my arms, the top of my head, and I am standing outside Mama's door. I call and call, but she does not answer.

When I wake, they lay me down, the men. Rest now, they say, and they climb out of the hole where they have put me, and cover up the opening with a boulder. I push myself up to a sitting position, drawing my knees to my chest. I cannot feel the cold, but I can taste it. Sweet as honey. And when I call Mama for the last time, I imagine she will come and take me in her strong, fat arms. And now? Now, I have eyes that let the moonlight through, as I crouch here, beside you, one who lies on this bed, so quiet, so still, whose hair falls across the pillow like the river at night.

Speak. Speak to me, one who lies on this bed.

Once, outside, beyond the bamboo reeds, the leaves moved, and so did I.

She appears through the darkness of the room where she hid me, the light of the lamp guiding her way. Her free hand clutches the heavy skirt of her dress, and her shoes click on the floor as she moves from the open door to the opposite wall, where she comes to a stop, her eyes falling on you first. She pushes her shoulders back a little, and takes a deep breath, as though gathering her strength to speak. She shakes her head. Answering a question only she can hear. Then she smiles, her tongue edging out to wet her bloodless lips.

I am not going to become Lot's wife. I am not going turn to salt for being weak. I am not going to mourn forever, while you fuck your little whores in Paradise!

She places the lamp on the floor and steps forward, spreading her arms wide. She takes me into them, while I am still lying on your bed with the shadow of that thing crouching at my feet.

I am now in a standing position, my hands drawn up in protest, my head pressed to your true wife's heart, as she walks back towards the open door. I can feel the moist heat of her flesh against my spine, can smell the rich sweet scent of her perfume, as she descends into the house, which is flooded with light that streams through tall windows. She places me in the corridor, close to the first door through which I came when I entered your world, and now everything falls into darkness again as she throws a cloth over me and secures the painting.

I hear the quick light footsteps of the girl, and her soft voice as she questions her mother. Then she falls to her knees, pleading, as the final knot is tied. She begs to go with me, but your true wife does not answer. Her knees crack as she rises, and she tells her to leave me alone, the sound of her shoes retreating across the wooden floor. The girl's screams are ignored. After a few moments, she drags herself closer and presses her mouth to the place where she thinks my face lies. I can feel her breath on my shoulder as she speaks.

This morning, I recalled a moment with Papa, which I'd like to share with you.

We were still in Paris, in Vaugirard. It was a sunny spring day, sometime in March, because the girls were selling daffodils at the roadside. It was chilly in the shade though. The wind was tossing the waves across the Seine, and shaking the stiff bare branches of the trees, which were beginning to sprout lime green buds. Papa held my hand tight as we walked along the street, and I asked him, when the leaves come out, will I be big? Papa said it would take longer, that the leaves may have to come out at least ten times.

I said that when I was big, I would take care of him. I would cook butter-roast pork and salted parsnips. And he laughed. What a combination, he declared, and his laughter carried across the river and people turned to look, the ladies in their dark dresses, and the men in silk hats, clutching their wooden canes. They smiled and someone remarked, what a lovely little boy you have! Then Papa laughed even harder, which made me cry. I cast my mind back to those tears he wiped away with the back of his hand. I'm not a boy, I told him, adamant. It is because of your hair, he soothed. We need to keep it short to stimulate the growth. But one day, my darling, when you are grown, you will have long dark tresses like your grandmother, who is descended from the Queen of Peru. What is Peru? I asked him.

But, oh, here comes Maman! She is sending you away to Paris where every man will set his eyes upon you. I am sorry to see you go and I will miss you. When you see Papa, please tell him I remember and that I have not forgotten my promise.

My mother was half Indian, half Inca, half Savage, so, you see, we are connected you and I.

I'm hungry.

There's still some bread left and a tin of corned beef.

We eat the same thing everyday.

Well, why don't you go out and catch us some fish then?

I hate you!

Drink some more absinthe then you'll love me again, won't you?

Ask your landlord for more food.

If I go, I'll be stuck there, you know how he likes to discuss...

White women?

And how they like to be seduced.

How do they?

They like to talk.

You like to talk.

Intelligence is too spiritual for me.

You like them fat and vicious.

Correct. Now go. And take this painting with you.

Is that you?

He says to accept it as payment for rent.

For the last six months?

It's called The Seed of the *Areois*.

You are brave to sit naked beside the river.

I didn't, I sat in his hut on a stool then he imagined me on a stone boulder and placed the flowering seed of the *hutu reva* in the palm of my hand, in the background there is Mount Arorai on one side and Orohena on the other, I'm supposed to be Vairaumati.

He has quite an imagination.

He is a genius and one day the world will know it.

What is a genius?

I am not sure.

Take it back, and tell him he can pay when his money arrives, hopefully on the next ship, the picture is not decent and will only be used for firewood like the last one, are you hungry?

Dear Diary,

Papa has managed to secure a free passage home with the help of the French Consul in Tahiti and will bring with him all forty paintings he has made during his time there. He is leaving the first week of August. Two years have flown by like a flash of lightening, but how painful they have been, the days, and weeks dragging at a snail's pace. I truly believed I would never see him again.

It will take him three whole months on the ocean waves to reach Europe and when he disembarks at Marseille, he will make straight for Paris and the Durand-Ruel where Vollard is awaiting him. He has been promised a solo exhibit. Papa is terrified and thrilled at the same time because, he says, he has left his peers and Post-Impressionism far behind, even those still attached to the school of Cloisonnism. He has created a new way of seeing which he calls Symbolism. He says it will revolutionise the art world. He has asked Maman to join him in Paris with *Manao Tupapau* but she refuses and has already had the painting shipped off to Monfreid.

It is strange, but now I am parted from her, I am bereft. She became a friend to me, of sorts, a thorn in my flesh I did not want to pull out. I have grown used to her presence. She would listen to me with that inscrutable gaze, never uttering a word of protestation. I wish I could go with her and wait there, in Paris, for Papa's arrival. I am finding it hard to sleep these past nights for thinking of his impending return, powerless to affect the tide and flow of events. When everyone is tucked up in bed, I make my nightly journey, one hand clutching my lamp, the other, the cross. Yes, I am still afraid of the *nisser* who like to hide in attics, and I scold myself as I go, telling myself – you are not a baby anymore! They do not exist!

We used to wait up, C and I, on Christmas Eve, promising one another to stay awake in order to catch a glimpse of the Yule Man. We would make sure Maman left out a bowl of rice pudding for him and a saucer of milk for his pointy-eared helpers. But we always fell asleep, to find the milk gone the next day and the pudding eaten, not one sticky grain left.

There's always a strip of light at the bottom of C's door. When I peer through the keyhole, I cannot see him, but I can Papa's painting, lit by the lamp on C's desk. Papa painted it when C was five, when he had long curly hair like a girl. C is fast asleep on the kitchen table, his golden locks falling down over his shoulders, the tips of his outstretched fingers touching Papa's tankard, filled with the malt beer he so loved. But the tankard is bigger than it actually is, gigantic in fact, and C, a tiny figure beside it.

I ask Papa for a taste, pulling at his trouser leg and he relents, placing his tankard down on the flagstones to pick me up in his arms. I am sitting on Papa's knee and all is right with the world. He clicks open the lid, and keeping it open, puts the edge of the tankard to my mouth, letting me have a sip. I don't like it, I don't like it at all, and I shake my head, quivering with disgust. Papa smiles, and nods to himself thinking he has taught me a lesson by allowing me to taste something forbidden. I press my face to Papa's chest, not wanting to climb down from his lap, and I listen to the hammering of his heart, which sounds far away, even though it is near. Papa smells of unwashed clothes, of bed linen stuffed into a wooden chest and forgotten about, which must be aired under the morning sun.

Is Papa sitting beneath the blazing sun now? Is she sitting beside him in her bare feet? Does she kneel? Does she have her head upon his lap and not his pillow? Is she weeping because he is about to leave? Do her tears wet his trouser leg? Does he take her face in his hands and tell her to stop?

You are free to go, to do as you wish. I don't believe in caging birds.

The sky is one half of a shell, in which Ta'aroa lived, in which he waited, folded, into himself.

The sky is a pale blue cloth pulled tight between four pillars that hold up this world.

The sky is made of hard rock crystal, and tied to this world with ropes. When the ropes break, our world will come tumbling down. And everything will be as if we never existed. For water will cover us. Water will cover me.

I'm going back to France, you say, we can't carry on like this. There's been nothing, no news, for more than six months now. I'll be back before you know it, a richer man.

I am free, to do as I wish, to step outside, to speak, to bare my teeth. But I stay, a while longer, to watch you pack, pull, cover, tie, open, lock, and carry your things from the doorway to the edge of the road, where the coach patiently waits, as I once did, on your bed, every inch of me.

You have given me ten francs as a leaving gift and made me promise to go straight home when I get off the coach at Taravao. So, how am I free?

I will return to my Foster Mother in the same dress I wore when I followed you here. When I said yes. Yes, yes, no. No, to being afraid, when I watched you spread my *pareu* across your bed, when you asked me to take off my dress, when you told me, we have time.

You will climb aboard one of the ships anchored in the bay of Papetee, on the other side of the island. You will stand on the deck, with more creases on your brow, your skin like old cloth, and the picture of me in the blue and white striped dress will lie under your feet, buried in the belly of a boat without an outrigger. You carry your ancestors in your eyes, you said, and this is what I want to capture, and you made me day after day, until I was finished.

You will sail quietly away, back across the circle of the sea, back to your true wife, and your fatherless children, and to the ones you call The Hypocrites, the ones you need recognition from. When I asked you what *recognition* meant, you said, to be recognised is like walking into a temple of statues and they all come alive for you.

She pleads from just outside our hut, from beyond the door, behind the wall, from the edge of their verandah. Come back!

When are you coming back? We have grown to love you! You promised to stay, but now you are leaving, never to return, is that not true?

You try to soothe her, promise you will return, that your soul remains here and this is where you wish to die. You wipe away the tears, and kiss the gurgling child in her arms, and her *tane*, your landlord, tells you he wants to give you a piece of earth in their very own burial ground, beyond the white pines.

I cannot see it, but I imagine the ground is soft, just as his voice is.

You do not place your hand on my back today. It is not laid out flat for you, but rigid and upright, because I am not asleep, because your work is done and you have caught the worm.

You will not wake me by pouring water over my face, will not tease and taunt me by bringing sweet tea fortified with absinthe.

I have grown used to these things.

I am a seed grown to the size of a boulder, pressed up against your flimsy reed walls. My toes poke out between the gaps, and the crown of my head grazes your leaf roof. Soon, I will burst open, push up through the light, which penetrates and pulses like the river, above me, all around. I can hear the sharp claws of the stray dog as he scratches, and whines, wanting to be let in, but today, there is no opening. None.

He sighs, finally giving up, and lies down on his front, his long thin legs splayed out before him, and he cleans his paws with a tongue the colour of a juicy *fei* roasted a dark orange.

The women leave their huts in silence.

They climb the mountain to find their ancestral *marae*. They are not supposed to do this, but they go, they disobey, they pretend, they forget. They wear the white man's cloth, the dresses they've just worn to Church so as not to arouse suspicion, and when they speak, when they do, it is a whisper.

One woman asks, who will speak this, what has happened, is happening now, in every village, in all the islands? But no one replies, because the answer is too raw, still a wound. Someone begins a chant, a song.

And Oro is called down from the mountain, from his peak, called down by his many names.

'Oro-i-te-maro-ura!
  'Oro-i-te-maro-tea!
  'Oro-pa'a!
  'Oro-rahi-to'o-toa!

Oro-of-the-red-feather-girdle!
  Oro-of-the-yellow-feather-girdle!
  Oro-fearless-warrior!
  Great-Oro-of-*toa*-wood!

Foster Mother carries the girl's broken body from the belly of the ship, onto the deck, towards the bow, where she finally opens her eyes.

She glimpses an infinite palace of nails that were treasures once.

I will speak this, she says, the girl who has grown to the size of a boulder, immense, inside the walls of The Painter's hut, which has become a windowless room, one without a door, without light.

I will, she repeats, I will give it words, and she smiles, her face glowing with an assurance unfamiliar to her and he sees it, The Painter, sees her smiling, seated upon their bed, with her back erect, like a newly sprung stem, hands placed one over the other, palms facing upwards, fingers curled to the shape of a bowl.

That face, he thinks, so precious. Precocious. What did you say? he asks. But she does not reply and he does not pursue his line of questioning, because, today, he has other things on his mind. He takes one last look at the letter, which grants him his ticket home. Then, he informs her it is time.

I am leaving now.

Oro looked everywhere for a lover, in all the islands. From Porapora to Maupiti, he looked, and from Maiao to Tahiti, but he could not find himself a girl worthy enough. Oro gave up his quest, and told his sisters – search for me – then flew back up to his mountaintop in a pillar of fire.

Teuri and Haoaoa looked in every village and every hut, on every island. In all the valleys and groves they searched, before they would also admit defeat. On the seventh day, they were about to return to Oro's peak, when they saw her, balancing on a boulder, which was anchored in the midst of a wide green river.

They could not see her face at first, only her long black hair, which fell down her back, and strong slender arms, outstretched to keep her steady. A pareu was tied low around glistening hips.

Then, she dipped forward and dived into the water like a yellow-beaked, white-and-black-feathered masked booby, letting out a cry of ecstasy. Cold, cold, she said, it is cold! And she swam with ease to the other side of the bank. Only then did she reveal her face, which was more beautiful than any tiare blossom. They found out her name was Vairaumati.

Orotetefa turned himself into a sacred red feather and Urutetefa took the form of a sow to celebrate their brother's union, as was the custom, and requirement of the god's two brothers. The earth and the ocean resounded with the cries of their coupling, god and girl, and all over the island, people listened at their doorways, on their mats, as did the birds in the trees. Then, one day, the land grew silent and Vairaumati's belly grew round and taut as a half moon in the night sky.

Oro loved Vairaumati, only to leave her and return to his mountaintop, this time on the back of a rainbow. But she did not mourn his leaving, Vairaumati. She gave birth to Tane, with her lover's promise echoing inside her skull – you will become mother of all of Tahiti.

You are my *tane* and I am your *vahine*. Am, was, yours. And now?

Who am I? What am I? And where am I going?

You said I was a handsome woman, never once did you call me beautiful.

You said it was my strength of character that drew you to me. It was my mind you loved. I challenged your assumptions. Arguing with you was fun. Dear god, we were both so young.

You only ever did three paintings of me. Don't you think that hurt? Made me feel small, insignificant, compared to the others, those girls who are not forgotten, and whose names I speak in the darkness, alone. But you are my wife, you protested. I come home to you!

As if that made everything right. I cannot help how I feel. It was always one humiliation after another, the servants talking behind my back, feeling sorry for me. Calling me stoic.

I wore the mask well, didn't I? Then to appease me, you carved my head in white marble, and inscribed your name on my lower lip. See, you proclaimed, my breath on your mouth, forever. You cried when you came, I remember, as if it were yesterday. We shared the same bed, sweat and tears. I possessed all of you, even your dreams, yes, and you possessed me too.

When the eldest was born, your eyes shone with gratitude, and you told me, this is first of the flesh of our flesh. And I imagined, foolishly, that we would always be, through this act, connected you and I, and the children would bind us together, closer for all time.

But she found me out, didn't she?

Found you out, one of your dirty little secrets. Told me what's what in no uncertain terms, the envelope marked, Paris, France. A second girl born to you when you were half way to Paradise, the flesh of your flesh...

The girl in white closes the gate to the big house and turns to face the square. The buttons on her dress, which begin where her collarbones meet and end at her waist, are mother of pearl, the shape of tears, uneven. The girl in white weaves her way around the women who sell their wares, who squat with ease, the hem of her dress arching over their bright flowers and fruits.

They are stunned by her audacity, the hawkers that belong to the market place. How dare she, they think, leaving the house before the sun has brought the shadows to bear. She clutches her folded note, the size of a fan. On reaching the wooden bench, she adopts the one empty space, not meeting the eyes of the other girls. She opens her note, quietly reciting the words contained within:

I will have a dress of every colour, and it will not matter that my skin is the shade of the earth.

The company she keeps, think her gone mad. The girl in yellow does not possess a note. She wipes the palms of her hands on her stained dress, and rises, walking towards the trees. They resemble the naked trunks of the fishermen, their long dark torsos. She carries on walking past them, towards the ocean, which throbs beneath the unbearable heat.

The Gendarme's Wife opens her front door and eases herself down the steps with the help of a wooden cane. She moves slowly over the florescent-green grass, a silhouette in her navy-blue dress. She comes to a stop at the closed gate, her eyes scanning the square, her gaze resting on the girls. She is only interested in the girl in white, her pale hand shielding the sun from her shrunken face.

They're all the same, he once said, The Painter, as he tugged her back across the square to the trap that waited with its horses. He told her, these women are fearful of what you represent, they are jealous of what they can never have, which is the freedom that lies at the very heart of you.

Through the long grass she had gone, and over the damp earth, leaving behind the imprint of her impatient feet.

Listen, Teha'amana, Foster Mother whispers, but her words are meaningless, just vibration, like water through a blowhole, a sacred song in the womb. The child, this child, a living gift, clings fast to the nipple, only interested in the sweet food it gives.

All that she is, and will be, the life she might live remains hidden now behind paper-thin lids, which are dark half moons, framed by a ring of thick black lashes. Her gaze is cast downwards, inverted, head inside heart she exists in a land of bliss, taking from its source, her nectar, and one true joy.

When she has finally had her fill, when she opens her eyes wide, and deigns to look up, she spies a goddess-like creature, towering above her, impenetrable, implacable; a bristling stone monument on a hill.

Foster Mother knows already, this girl of hers, will become, not a woman, but a collector of experiences.

I hope you are listening, my daughter, she says. I want to tell you, so it seeps into your being, before you understand its meaning. I want to tell you about the world and how it was truly made.

Teha'amana turns to face the wall, the bamboo reed wall. She is older by a year, and a day. She peers through the long thin gaps towards the light, the creaking light.

She strains to hear the ocean beyond, on the other side of the road, because her Foster Mother's hut is mountainside. She grasps it, or imagines she can. She is good at imagining now, an expert. It flows, silent as a heartbeat, her imagination, and the ocean too.

The wind moves through the leaves outside, and it reminds her of the pages of his book, the one he kept hidden, and pulled out at night. The one he scribbled in when he thought she was sleeping.

He will tell the world she was older by two years to make their affair more palatable. She would like to open her wings and fly round the world without stopping once to take rest. But she is not an albatross.

The rain begins to fall. Does not stop. It pours, pounds on the roof, their *pandanu* leaf roof. She lies on her mat, still turned to the wall, thankful. Grateful.

She is finally home, but ripe with grief, for some reason not known to her. Yet she knows her Foster Mother watches. And she listens to her every movement, her slow, wide feet as they cross the dirt floor, her impatient breath, the strong hands, which lay powerless on her lap. Foster Mother ventures to ask, do you want to get up and try on your new dress?

The bamboo creaks. The door opens. The world is white, colder than the seawater at dawn, when the sun hasn't warmed it through, colder than the lakes high up on the plateaus where the red-bellied ducks like to bathe, where they hide. She jumps in. Slides in. Falls headlong.

She walks along a path, passing two farmhouses made of stone and flint. It is the place he promised her she would be happy,

Le Pouldu. I will take you there, he'd said, and you will be at home, I know you will. The granite echoes dully under her clogs.

The girls wait on the wooden bench in Taravao, their dresses sewn tight to their forms, their eyes darting back and forth, past the jewelry sellers, the fruit sellers, and the fishermen. The girl in yellow gets up now and walks to the edge of the market place where The Gendarme waits. She follows him through the gate, the soles of her feet dusty, dirty, and she disappears into the shadows of the big house.

It is not one of those girls. And it is not the one in the city, when he lived alone, where he was lonely. Not the girl he shared with the men whose names she forgets, except Degas, because he spoke this name in his sleep. No, it is not Olympia, but the one who wears the white cloth hat of a peasant girl and wide starched collar, the one who pushes her toes into shoes carved from the trunk of a birch tree, who pins a crimson rose to the strap of her apron, and who interlaces her fingers with the other peasant girls and dances for him.

Later, she will take off her dress and petticoats and lie down on a cliff top. She will press her spine into the grass, black as the hair between her legs, and she will look up at a solemn sky with one long cloud in it, like an opening. And she listens to the villagers coming home from the wedding, drunk on apple cider. Yes, it is the one who holds the yellow-eyed fox to her luminous breast, and in her other hand, between thumb and forefinger, she holds the stalk of a red-tipped cyclamen.

And she lies like that in his picture of loss, hidden, hiding their secret.

There are two of you now.

But. I don't want it inside me.

A child is the most precious gift.

He made me lie naked, made me sit down on the floor of his hut, on a rock beside the river, in a forest clearing.

It is finished now.

I don't want it inside me.

Hina went to Tefatou and asked him, begged him, to let man live, to never allow him to die. But Tefatou, in his arrogance, in his grace, Tefatou, the one who manifests the earth, whose voice resonates in the world below, refused her request.

He gave this reasoning:

Plants must die. All vegetation, after their time of growth, of blooming, of giving, must return to the earth. It is the natural order of things, and man in correlation must also wither and die. It is so, and will be, forever more.

Hina, disgruntled by his decision, replied, do you as you wish, but I will cause the moon to be reborn every month.

The ship floats, steers silently, moving across the endless empty seas, for days, weeks, years, a century, and a half, until one day, it finally reaches its stop.

A voice begins, sonorous. The first sentence is laid down, like an offering then repeated. Another voice joins, softening the refrain. A second sentence emerges, its words flung up to the gods.

All the voices come together now, man, woman, child, separate yet united, in the perfect utterance of all things past.

And the past rises up into the wide domed roof of their communal hut, lulling to sleep the stray dogs that have dared to venture inside and have not been chased away. The oil lamps burn steadily at the opening but it is the fullness of the moon that lights the path for the spirits within. This is not a discussion of one of the lessons contained within The Gospel. It should be, and yet it is not.

Foster Mother sits at the outer edge of the group of women, in the furthest corner from the doorway, her hunched form melting into the semi-darkness. Beside her, Teha'amana crouches, her weary head grazing her second mother's shoulder. My child, Foster Mother thinks, her stomach contracting with guilt and grief, my girl, whom I took for my own, and named for strength.

I brought you here to clean you, to make you well, make things right because it is not, and cannot be, too late. I did what I thought, what I believed was best.

They lie entwined like two vine leaves, his belly hot against her spine, his breath soft against her ear.

She recalls him kissing her, Teha'amana, when she should not be thinking of that now, here, in this hut of songs, but she does.

He caresses her as she lays on her front, kisses her inch by inch, all the way down, from the point her skull bone meets her spine, to her tailbone, her coccyx.

He strokes her buttocks, and tells her he loves her even more today than yesterday.

Ta'aroa in his final throes of creation plucked the other gods from the darkness and made each one, god over each newly created thing. The animals of the earth, sky, and water became the messengers of these gods, the turtle, shark, and dove.

Ta'aroa passed his shadow over a breadfruit tree and from this act of union, Hina came into being, then he made love to her, his own child, and Hina gave birth to many, including Tii.

Tii lay down with Ani, and from them was born Desire of the Night, the messenger of shadows and of death, and Desire of the Day, the messenger of light and of life.

And from them, came Tii of the within, and Tii of the without. And from them, in turn arose happenings of the day and happenings of the night, the coming and going, the giving and receiving of pleasure.

I understand now, what forever means.

It means, tomorrow.

In the beginning, before you made me, before a piece of me was trapped forever in the rhapsody of your island, even before I was bone and blood and mind, before all the boats and what they brought, their gifts of death. I was a girl who walked out into the night, my feet tip-toeing damp soil, damp from the breath of sea, so near.

Can you hear me still, beating my *tapa* from the bark of a mulberry tree, for a god that does not want or appreciate my devotion? They are my eyes now, yours. You've written yourself into me, just as I am written into you, Teha'amana, Tehura, fire in the blood, hussy. Trollop. Eve.

You wonder what he felt when he entered you. For you, it hurt, but you would not say it, never said, though he carried on hurting you. A wooden bed, you thought, kept on thinking, a bed with good dreams that would bring me gifts, however bitter, it would be sweet, in time.

You allowed him to push you back against the cloth of your Foster Mother's *pareu*, dark blue with yellow petals, which you traced with one finger. You watched him spread it out before, then after the deflowering, you let him bruise you, before giving you your first pleasure then he licked away your tears, which fell, unannounced. He insisted on doing that.

He told you about his daughter, who would be your age now, then spoke of the sacrifice he'd made for the sake of his Art. You did not know what he meant by that, instead you drew your finger along his spine, the same finger that had traced the imprint of the *tiare* blossom on your mother's *pareu*, and you took in the bitter odour of his skin then pulled yourself from under him. He let you, the first and only time.

You can still feel the shadow of his hands on your wrists, and you remember the moment you opened your legs and guided him into you, because you knew there was no way back. Back to the completeness you'd felt sitting on the boulder at the river's edge with Taneipa, while the mosquitoes bit your arms and you slapped them away with languid irritation. She told you things in the silence of those days, as you both watched the eels twist themselves between one another in a slow dance. And excitement and dread tied themselves into a knot deep in your belly.

I want to tell you now. Tell you – you belong in the world.

He left knowing you did not love, that what you loved, truly, was beyond him, in your *fenua*, in the *makatea* surrounding your island, and it had put a fear in him and he thrust harder when he should have been gentle, he knew that.

You were eleven, just eleven, not thirteen, untouched before he touched the very core of you, and made the tangible, intangible. You listened, and you watched, but you did not speak. She does not speak, he told his landlord. You heard them from beyond the bamboo reed walls, but she will get down on her back for me, for the modest reward of a frock, or a pair of copper earrings. And you gripped the edge of your pillow where you lay exposed, and wrapped yourself around your *pareu* and rolled like that, onto the dirt floor. You lay on the ground, in your cocoon, still, wondering what you should do next. And you glimpsed the moon through the doorway, a pale shadow, sharing the sky with the sun.

He found you like that, fallen, took your face in his hands, and squeezed a little too tight, before kissing the tip of your nose, the crown of your head, then told you, be a good girl and take your position, the picture is nearly done, afterwards, we'll celebrate with a drink. And he put a new bottle of forgetting on the shelf beside the empty one. They are my eyes now, yours. You have written yourself into me, just as I am written into you. I am Hina – do you hear?

Can you hear, the sound of my mallet, beating beautiful white *tapa* for a god that does not require my devotion?

The Missionary sways from side to side like a giant purple hibiscus flower, the cross on his chest glinting, made of the metal white men think so precious, which you said lived in my skin, and you caught it many times, in your hands, your gold, in the light of the lamp. They say he does not take it off, the cross, even when he climbs into bed, naked as a baby.

Sister stands beside him, deep shadows under her eyes, hands in the same place as before, one over the other against the brown cloth of her dress, when she told me, we are powerless – she and I.

And through the open window, the mountains rise up in silence, rose up through the darkness, when the world was made.

The Missionary's hairless head shines with sweat, and swollen fingers pull from his sleeve, a folded square of white cloth. He wipes his brow from side to side then presents it, a soiled note to Sister. Lips twitching, she accepts, sliding it into the hidden compartment of her skirt. She looks up nervously, to see if anyone has seen. We read her and she reads us, and I wonder what is written across the pages of her book?

The Missionary pushes his shoulders back, lifting the small chin out from a trunk-like neck, and looks carefully at the congregation spread out before him. The men are seated to one side, and the women on the other. He asks someone, anyone – can you describe this Hell, the place in which the *Areois* now live?

And he waits, like the priest used to wait on the *marae*, once, a long time ago, with a plucked eye in the palm of his hand, an offering to the mighty Ta'aroa.

You call this one Words of the Devil. Then you place the words in the earth, which you make the colour of flesh. *Parau na te Varua ino* lies beneath your name and the numbers nine and two. This you tell me is how old the world is, its age since His death, because it was only born after His dying, and you open the old wounds on your legs with your scratching, cursing the mosquitoes that love your blood.

You have made it so I am clutching a square of white cloth to my nakedness. It covers my sex, just, and I hold my other hand up, the tips of my fingers at my jawline in a gesture of surprise. I look behind me, my eyes straining sideways, to the back of my head, where our bed stands. You have imagined the shadow there, kneeling, at the edge of the forest, beside a clump of bright red hibiscus flowers, whispering, with lips of coral, this is what she says:

I can describe this Hell in which the *Areois* live, where the flames climb so high, they block out the sky. The women are tied to one another with ropes of iron, and they take it in turns to feed the fire, to keep it burning, at every hour of every day, except there are no days in Hell, but an endless night. Their gleaming skin, once oiled with the scent of coconut and *tiare* blossom is now black with soot and the heat of the smoke. And they roast like this, the women, like wild boar on a spit, just for the amusement of the Devil.

The bell rings out across Faaone, again, and again, inspiring fear in the ones it calls to action. Sister strikes it with measured abandon, and with each strike, she whispers – wake, wake up, rise, and shake the cobwebs from your mind.

She stands beneath the herald of The Word, taking pride in the fact she alone brought it from Lyon across the arduous seas. She was entrusted with its care, with the mission of installing it, and remembers the excitement she had felt at being the purveyor of the call to prayer, the knot she had felt, that she feels, in her gut each time, on the Sabbath Day, when she walks those eighty eight steps, towards the task of striking it, of making the bell sing, cry out.

Her lustrous hair, concealed beneath her habit, was once the colour of the fruit of the *mape* that grow further upriver. The wide sleeve of her dress has fallen down to her elbow to reveal the sun-neglected arm of a young woman, an arm that carries upon it, many layered scars, cuts that were made with the tip of a gold edged quill. Healed now by years of abstinence, forgiveness, and God's love.

She pauses for a few minutes, waiting for the savages to come hither. She knows after a short while, she must strike the bell again, harder this time, to make them pull on their clothes, their eyes now open, their conscience awakened, their dreams broken. They will realise they are naked, she thinks, and they will be ashamed.

She wants to heal them, though she knows it is perhaps too late for her, the girl, Teha'amana.

Sister's eyes widen in surprise at my description of Hell, and she meets my look with wonder, a smile softening her thin lips. I hold her gaze until she breaks it, her cheeks flaming, she turns away to pick up the chalk. She writes on the board, 'Lesson for Today, The 7th Commandment'. The Missionary narrows his eyes, anger flashing through the blue, all the wisdom of the world in his beak, ready to spill. And after a small silence, he addresses me, directly.

To woman, the Lord God said, I will greatly multiply your sorrow, and in sorrow you shall bring forth children, and your desire shall be to your husband, and he shall rule over you.

Then he turns to Sister, her white fist floating, waiting, and gives the signal to begin with a nod of his head. He falls into the chair made of the same rosewood as the door through which we enter, and through which we will leave. He closes his eyes like the one behind him, who hangs high above, and I wonder if the stars were also born at the time of His dying. I take hold of my Foster Mother's hand and my Birth Mother's who sits on the other side of me. I do not look at either of them but their grip tightens, reassuring, comforting.

The lesson for today is the seventh commandment. Thou shalt not kill. First, we will repeat the previous commandments as a reminder. One. I am the Lord thy God and I have brought thee out of the house of bondage.

We take off our garlands of wild mountain blossom and place them on the wooden stool. We sit down on the earth packed floor. My copper earrings spin, caressing the sides of my neck, silently. They are the shape of coins, but thin as leaves.

You were furious because I made you buy them then I never wore them again. No, I am not like other girls.

Two. Thou shalt have no other gods before me.

We tear the baked breadfruit with our hands, our dark fingers, all thirty of them. Content, Ta'aroa gazed at the world he had created and everything in it was pleasing to him. The shadow of his thought fell on a young breadfruit tree. From this union, Hina was born, his daughter, lover. Helper.

Three. Thou shalt not make unto thee any graven image.

She did not want to take me in her arms when I was born, my first mother, in case her heart would cling. It still clings. I possess her eyes, her nose, her mouth, even the song of her voice, but my thoughts are my own, and I am not like her. She wanted these wide, thick fingers to be long and tapered, my second mother, like a white woman's, delicate and full of grace, but they did not turn out that way. I did not turn out that way.

Now, with their bellies half-full, Foster Mother plucks the bottle of *kava* from the shadows and passes it to her cousin sister, my Birth Mother. She pushes the rest of the breadfruit towards me. Eat, she says with tenderness, but it is a command. They pass the bottle between them, my mothers, sipping, sighing, and watching my every movement with curious eyes, with eyes that strip me bare.

But they find nothing to tell them what they know and knowing what will come, they drink some more, drink the whole bottle, every last drop, to forget, because tomorrow is another day.

Thou shalt not kill. Thou shalt not. Thou shalt.

Not.

He has enlisted the help of a man of letters, one who follows his own school of thought, to transform his diaries into a work of fiction. It will describe his journey to the heart of Paradise, a symbolic shedding of skin of all he once knew. His ego knows no bounds.

He has forgotten all about me of course, though he acknowledged my presence each time he passed beneath me, and once, in real life, he knelt before me with hollow eyes and eager hands. On the day of our departure, he unpinned me from my place above the doorway and thrust me between the pages of one of his books.

Now, here I am, in complete darkness, where I can hardly breathe. Paper, dried ink and his words are all I can taste. I'm stuck between the account of his fishing-trip and his return home to his *vahine*. Once again, he has taken liberties with the details of that day, when in truth, this is what actually transpired...

She collected fallen twigs, bark, and coconut husk to build a fire and began preparing the fish he'd brought back with him. She asked for the knife he'd used to fashion her wooden face. She baked his portion over the open flames because he liked it that way and took hers raw. He watched her chewing for some time then ventured to say, all artists are cannibals too. She did not reply or even look up, but carried on chewing, like a haughty queen, or a statue upon an altar. Expressionless. Her silence angered him further, and in order to elicit a response, he asked, have you been faithful today?

She turned her gaze towards him then, her eyes blacker than the shadows all around them. Finally, she spoke.

I have been drying *pandanus*, can you not see, over there? The leaves are still hanging on the branch of the tree. I want to make a fan, if I can remember how, the way my mother—But he was not listening and intervened. He informed her, the fish had spoken.

She swallowed the last morsel of flesh upon her tongue and with a sigh, knelt down before him. She replied with resignation, that is an old superstition, but if you believe it, then you must do what is right, and she held his look through a veil of sadness, or perhaps, it was wisdom?

Then he also knelt down before her and took her face in his hands and said he could not. That he did not believe she would have been unfaithful. Just because his hook pierced his *tunny* through the lower jaw does not mean his *vahine* was unfaithful while he was away. Those fishermen like to gossip and create a stir. Yes, they are probably jealous of him, of them. She nodded, relieved, shut her eyes, and fell back against the floor of the hut, holding her arms out to receive him, and eagerly, obligingly, he covered her body with his own. Tears fell, disappearing into the dried earth, which held them both, the lovers.

How cunning she has become. Of course, I knew better. I'd watched her, earlier the same day, lead a boy with a face as duplicitous as her own onto their bed, and like the words in this diary, on another page, she showed him how to touch her, by drawing her claws through her own furry skin.

The *mape* tree clings to the river, to the banks, to the edge of the forest, solemnly reaching, stretching downwards.

Its leaves are as large as the palm of her hand, rounded, dark green with veins of orange. The roots are wide, exposed, rising up through the soil, shoring the trunk of the tree on all sides, protruding from the shallow earth like curved, curving walls. She crouches between two roots, now very small, in miniature, the size of a rock dove, except she has no feathers.

They have all been plucked out, and she is naked once more, head drawn down between her knees, a mute. She breathes in her own scent, and it is something she recognises but cannot place, sickening. She cranes her neck to take in the lower branches and breathes in the purity of the flower of the *mape*, five-petal, white, and pale yellow.

She picks up a fallen fruit that has turned a brown-orange hue. It is overripe, a section of it fallen away with decay, and she prods out the kernel with one finger. She bites into it, knowing it is poison. Knowing it must be cooked first, and remembering how they once prepared it, her and Taneipa, grated and mixed with coconut milk into a pulp then baked in banana leaves, until it was soft, and sticky sweet.

The sore between her legs, on her sex, is raw. It hurts like knives down there, and she cannot rise, finds it impossible to walk. She must crawl, like this from the roots of the *mape* to the edge of the water.

She bites again into the chestnut kernel.

This is her dream.

After a silence of two days, Foster Mother places the palm of her hand on my back, and says – she has gone to the heart of Papenoo, to live the old way, with the others who have also gone there, her *tane*, one of them.

I imagine the white man's cloth does not adorn her proud body, Taneipa. She wears her *pareu* tied loosely around her waist, her shoulders, breasts, and arms, bare under the warming hands of the sun. She watches her daughter crawl in the earth, also naked, and happy.

The women squat beside her like a pair of coconut crabs, breaking shells. Their hair, their skin is fragrant with *monoi*. The women watch their men scale the tall trees in the distance, nimble as the rats that climb them at night. And they scrape the white pulp from the inside of the nut. They will dry it out to make their precious oil, scenting it with honey-sweet blossom gathered across the mountainside.

She presses the tips of her fingers to her scalp, Taneipa, and massages it in small circles, letting out deep sighs of satisfaction. She closes her eyes and remembers how she did this for me, and how I did it for her, and she may regret telling me once Hina does not inhabit the moon. Or she may not dwell on the life before this one because she is young and everything breathes of the present, of this day.

Not of what is to come, or the world beyond this valley, which belongs to the white man.

Late, at night, she will cry out like a bird caught in a tree. She will unclasp her legs from around the thighs of her *tane*, and they will lie beside one another on their mat, looking up into the darkness of their *pandanu* leaf roof, and she will quietly tell him this:

Once, The Missionary told us our feelings live above the left breast, where the heart beats. But I know, knew then, feelings live in the belly, where babies grow.

And she will turn to look at their sleeping child and her *tane* will curl his strong body around hers, his hand resting on the place where more life is to come.

The next morning she will carry their daughter towards the *marae* that remains intact, because the white man has not dared venture this far. She will wait beyond the border wall, because it is *tapu* for women to enter inside, and she will keep sacred the rites of our ancestors.

And she will not question the blood that was once spilled, on a leaf plucked from the *miro* tree, on the black stones, the cornerstone, the altar.

And she may think of me, her little sister, may wonder, if my toes, the soles of my feet, my palms, the insides of my thighs, my shoulder blades, my arms, my wrists, my neck, the back of my neck, my sex, if all of me has been touched by the white man, the one who makes human beings with colour. And she may regret the day she came to find me, full of joy, here, beside the green river, when she said, go quick, when she said, you are lucky.

Does she remember? Does she dream of finding me, of stepping outside the valley, of coming here to this place, by the water's edge, where I am waiting?

How long the days have become, without their presence, their essence, *iho*, his breath on hers, no words, hardly any words, just the heat of two living souls, and the beat of the human heart. I miss the sound of his work, day after day, as soon as the sun rose he would begin, until it fell, like a burrowing, and her patience growing in that time, tall and wide, reaching into the darkness of the roof above, like the branches of a tree.

Once, I watched their story unfold, from my place high up in the eaves. Now, I wonder where she has gone, where she lies, with those eyes, which he cut out of wood, and painted black.

On the last day, she pulled on the dress in which she had entered the hut, pink, faded almost to white, too tight, skimming the bottom of her thighs. She wrapped The Good Book in her blue and yellow *pareu* and threaded the copper earrings back into her lobes, then returned like that, just as she had arrived. Almost.

We both grieve, the hut and I, the bedframe the only object that has not been dragged back to the landlord's house. How naked these walls seem, now they are not covered with his treasured postcards and pictures, sources of inspiration torn from the pages of the *Mercure*. She is gone too, his Olympia, from her place above the doorway, and I don't miss her, even a little. There is one picture I miss though, and thinking about it makes me quite melancholic, because I will never know that world, and would perish in such conditions.

The landscape is buried in a sea of white, a white so white there are hints of blue to its edges. The trees stand defeated, stripped of their clothes, and the rivers and lakes are bound in a vow of silence. I will never taste the sharpness of the air beneath those grey skies, just as she, his *vahine*, will never climb the shimmering hills, which rise to sharp peaks in the distance.

The bedframe stands alone in the middle of their deserted hut, now just a yawning memory. The mattress has been dragged back to the landlord's house, and thrown down across his verandah, where a baby now plays, where he coos like the ground doves that greet the men who come off the boats in Papeete. And who leave.

It stands abandoned, the bedframe, like the insides of this place, when not long ago, it held them within it, across, between.

It is the one object that made up her mind when she entered his hut, a simple hut of bamboo reed and *pandanu* leaf, disappointment enveloping her like a thick cloak of feathers. She did not say it out loud, but to herself she said: At least you have a proper bed.

One made of good wood, with four legs that hold it up, to separate my dreams from the earth, the dirt floor, that is something. Even though you live in a hut no bigger than the one I grew up in. Even though you have taken The Good Book, and placed it high up on a shelf, out of my reach. Even though, your walls are covered with human beings that belong to your world, not mine, and who look down at me, through me, with eyes that do not move. But I know they are alive, and I will have to get used to it.

I ask if that is your country, the one covered in white, and you tell me yes, it is *wintertime*. It becomes very cold then, so cold the water of the lakes and the rivers stop flowing and the rain falls silently, softly, frozen, like tiny pieces of lace. This you call *snow*. On the hill, the women are feeding a fire. They are stoking the flames into being. You say they are doing this to roast a pig for the men when they return from the hunt. We do this too, I want to tell you, but the words disappear as soon as I open my mouth. To speak, to say, our women do this too.

Their feet sink into the *snow*. The dogs follow their masters, their noses pointing downwards, trying to catch the scent of living things, and of death. The hunters carry long wooden poles across their rounded shoulders, their faces hidden from me, like the secrets you kept, unlocked.

They are whistling as they go, the hunters, and their sound carries over the brow of the hill to the world below. Below, the people of the village gather across blue-gray squares, where the lakes have hardened. Some are holding hands, and laughing, turning round and around. The children are happy today. One has fallen down, and another is running from his mother with his arms outstretched.

Below, a woodcutter walks across a bridge, carrying a bundle of branches and twigs on his back. He stops to watch two girls crossing the river in their bare feet, their skirts pulled up to reveal pink-white legs. The frozen surface has broken here already and the water flows freely.

They are brave, he thinks.

Is he remembering a time when laughter floated down from the house on the hill where a fire now burns outside the door? Does the promise of food fill his empty belly, or is it love, the memory of his woman's face?

In *summertime* the trees will wake up and get their leaves again, and the hunters will return. They will push back their shoulders with pride and blow into their pipes. They will strike their drums, and their music will carry across the valley. It will spread its wings wide like the black bird in flight, a bird, which has tasted a place, many oceans away.

Will it hurt?
    I won't lie to you.
    How long will it take?
    Who is your *tane*?
    He has gone, back to his true wife.
    It will be over in the time it takes to walk to Taravao.

She guides me, naked, to the edge of a shallow pit, and delivers me into the care of another, whose hands are gentle, gentle and sure. She has the face of someone I could love, her eyes tender, her smile, softer.

Soft, and heavy, that is the sound of my heart, now it knows what has to be done to this body that belongs to it. My thighs tremble like a leaf, like two leaves.

You spread my *pareu* across the bed then place a thick white blanket over the top, which is pale blue underneath.

I brought it with me all the way from France, you say, from there to here. I lie down on my front, as I am told, then you tuck my hair behind my right ear spreading the ends out across the pillow.

I want to see the nape of your neck, you say. Then, you press the palms of my hands flat on the pillow either side of my face, cross my feet at the ankles, and tell me to stay like that while you make me.

You don't stop making me for three whole days in the same position. For three nights, you don't touch me as we lie, side by side. But when the sun falls on the fourth day, when it drops, exhausted, into the lagoon, you say, it's been long enough, I can't wait any longer for this painting to be finished. I've been good. My whole life I have been good.

Was it then, when it was made, the life inside?

Because, on the last day, while you were finishing my feet, the feet of the other me that now lives on a square of cloth pulled tight between a wood frame, in your imagined land, my blood, the blood of the real me began to trickle down the inside of one thigh. It doesn't matter, you said. Then, you came. Then, it stopped.

Bend both knees...let your legs fall open.

She pushes it in, up, as far as it will go then further still, to the very ends of this earth, the long white stem. I look. Look into the eyes of the kind one, and imagine I am lost there, in her good will, and I am small again. I am four. I am five. I am six. I am hers, her child alone. Until the pain stirs me back.

You trace the pattern on my *pareu*, from the stem to the leaf to the petal to my elbow, to my hand.

These hands that you make bigger than the soles of my feet, because you can. In your hut, on your bed, you place the palms of your hands on my back, kneading, pressing the flesh away, as though looking for something.

Finally, you give up, and lie down beside me, burying your words in my hair, while I keep mine hidden.

I was walking along a farm lane looking for a spot to set my easel down. It was only when I finished the scene, of sloping roofs, cottages surrounding a courtyard well, that I looked behind me, and saw a red barn door. I made a quick watercolour sketch of it before the light began to fade. The next day, I left for Arles. Later, I dreamt of that door. I was standing on the black rocks of Le Pouldu, looking out towards the horizon, where the door floated silently. I wanted to reach it, to enter inside, but as I swam nearer, it resumed its distance, like a trick of the light, pushing me deeper into the ocean. As my head began to sink into the depths, I woke up.

I know now Tahiti was that door, the red door in my dream, and you were behind it, waiting.

Stop screaming, the whole island will hear.

This is what came out of you.

You can close your legs now.

They took, took, took all the gods, all twenty-four, and placed them inside the hollow of his body, the skull and bones of the queen who'd lain the first cornerstone abandoned somewhere on the mountain.

They took her from her tomb, inside his belly.

One of them broke off his penis in anger. See, he said, you have no power! And they laughed. Then two of them carried him, because he was the size of a nine-year old boy, but heavier, to the boat without an outrigger, where The Reverend Lancelot waited. He would take them to the sacred isle of their bloodline, and the home of The Missionary, John Williams.

They pushed him onto his back, against a piece of bark cloth, so that he faced the sky, defeated, now just a block of carved sandalwood, which the white men would call strange, and compare to a toad.

They would not tell their brethren he had been carved with devotion and a precision so fine, his entire body told the story of their creation.

He had been imagined with a stone-bladed chisel, sanded down with a shark's skin rasp, polished with breadfruit leaves and cowrie shells, and finished off with coconut oil, so that his skin gleamed like precious metal.

Each one, each one, each one of his helpers, thirty in total, the size of an ear, eye, nose, mouth, nipple, clung to his fragrant body, his golden torso, his limbs, with their arms spread wide, or folded, fast asleep. Once, they were, all of them, imbued with his *mana*.

They followed the white man to the house of The Missionary and his wife Mary, and did as they promised they would. They gave him over and in the giving over, the one who had broken off his penis said, here he is, A'a, we give him to you, because we are true to our word. And he would not, dare not say the name, Ta'aroa. Because a fear ran so deep, it was impossible to root out.

So, he said, here he is, A'a, we give him to you, we are true to our word. Just as the God our Father is true to his.

On John Williams' orders, they took all the gods out of his wooden form, and one by one threw them onto a specially built pyre, its flames leaping tall and bright outside the House of the Mission, under the shadow of Mount Temehani. Then, A'a, emptied, blinded, and violated, was carried back onto the boat, now light as a feather. But they did not see the one red feather, which was caught in a hairline crack, in a splinter within his trunk.

He would be carried, Ta'aroa, with his other name, part name, pseudonym. Carried all the way to England, to the country of Lancelot Edward Threlkeld and his glorious King.

Everything has a shell.

Man's shell is woman because he comes from her. And woman's shell is woman because she comes from herself.

Teeth, sharp as knives of iron, grow from the palms of her hands, from her fingertips, her chin, between the fine hair on her upper lip, across her cheeks, which are like two large islands separated by the wide bridge of her nose. Teeth appear from her broad wrists, from her watermelon breasts, Ranganua, the cannibal goddess, is all teeth.

She feasts on the trembling flesh of her daughter's lover, but she cannot find his heart, which has hidden itself under the bones, the blood, and the guts, from her deadly teeth, which have appeared all over her body in the act of eating.

Everyday, Ranganua goes out to catch tender young crab for Hina. She will only give her daughter the best of food to eat. She goes out at dawn, when the sun is still climbing, while her sweet girl sleeps, to the coral reef where these delicacies live, their pale flesh palpable beneath the translucent shell.

She can be seen at sunrise, moving across the crest of the waves, a shadowy figure, at the edge of the reef, waiting, patiently bent over.

After breakfast, as soon as her mother's weary eyes close, Hina escapes, hurrying out of their hut in the direction of the mountains, to the crown of the diadem, a monument to the cannibal queen herself. There, in a cave, her faithful lover waits, carefully concealed. Once inside their private chamber, Hina shares her food with him, whatever she has managed to keep aside, packed into her pareu. Then, with their bellies full, they lie down together.

Suspecting her daughter does not have such a large appetite, Ranganua decides to feign sleep one day and when Hina leaves their hut, she uses magic tricks to arrive at the diadem before her. She sits perched on the branch of a white pine in the form of the sacred vini bird and watches as Hina comes to a stop, breathless, beside a boulder covering the opening to a cave. She hears her daughter whisper the secret mantra that makes the stone door fall to one side and allow her in.

Ranganua spreads her scarlet wings, flaps them in flight and returns to foot of the valley, where their hut stands. She turns back into human form, and falls exhausted onto her mat.

Jealousy takes root. It clings to her heart, growing quickly, enveloping a once pure love.

The next day, instead of making her pilgrimage to the reef at first light, she returns to the diadem before Hina rises.

Languishing in a half dream, Hina believes she has been listening to her mother's early morning preparations to catch tender crab and so lets herself fall into a deeper sleep. It will be a day like yesterday, her heart tells her soul, and you'll soon be in your lover's arms, and he will enter you. And she presses the place between her legs, her body aching with undiminished desire for him.

Teeth grow from her hands, the palms of her smooth hands, from the virgin island that is her face, from the unmarked brow, the gentle chin, the bow of her upper lip, and she becomes, like her mother, all teeth. She feasts on the flesh of her beloved, but she cannot find his beating heart, because it has hidden itself, from her murderous fangs, from her ancestral teeth, which have appeared all over her body in the act of eating.

Hina wakes with a cry, her mat soaked with sweat, and does not stir until the sun, her friend, has nestled itself between the soft white clouds. With a deep sense of unease, Hina climbs the mountain, towards the diadem between Orohena and Arorai, and arrives outside the illicit chamber, where the boulder lies on the grass, revealing the opening. Inside, she does not find her lover, but the remains of him, his bones, in a pool of blood.

In the silence, she hears a heartbeat, not hers. It speaks faintly through the darkness, and she speaks back to it from the walls her grieving flesh.

A plume of smoke rises up into the sky, a sky the colour of cornflowers, weeds like jewels in the cornfields of his youth. On the wooden deck, he watches, his left eye pressed to the spyglass, borrowed from the ship's captain.

There she is, he tells himself, at the end of the pier, perched on the rocks, a dark figure drawn sharply against the sun, legs dangling, big sturdy feet trailing water. The flower I placed in her hair has fallen onto her lap. Yes, she's there amongst the faces gathered, the ones already mourning their lost lovers. They sing of a man who has left his family, who is to be found on the other island, languishing beneath the shade of his favorite tree, where the breezes from the South and the East come together, where they join.

He cannot remember the words exactly, but he has listened to the women sing it many times on the verandah of his landlord's house.

The ship rears its body, like a powerful beast, retreating. He can feel its weight beneath his old toes and cracked soles. He still walks barefoot, his shoes stolen in broad daylight from outside his door the first week of this stay. He never bothered replacing them. But now, he thinks, I must buy a new pair before I step back onto French soil.

He retrieves from his trouser pocket the souvenir he bought for his daughter in the market place. The coral, flesh pink, is the opposite colour of the sea today, which is a deep blue-green. The jewelry seller told him they came from the waters of The Marquesas. That is where I will go next, he thinks, when I return, the landscape unspoiled, like the girls.

And he holds it up higher, the necklace, and through the jagged pieces of rock he can see his island growing smaller. O Tahiti, he whispers.

And the ocean echoes his sentiment.

Is that you?

Yes, do you think it's a true likeness?

It could be any Maohi girl.

And you could be any boy.

What will you do when he leaves?

Marry you.

I'm promised to another, my mother's already bought ten hogs for the feast, and twenty chickens to slaughter.

Will you invite me?

No.

Kiss me then.

Did you know there's a house in France, which is full of ghosts, there are ghosts in every room, and they cling to the walls, the doors, to the shadows.

I know…it's a house with a hundred rooms, and you have to pass through to get there. France.

If your *tane* wants to take you and make you his true wife, will you go?

No, he's already made me a hundred times, here in this hut.

What do you want then?

I don't want to die. I'm too young. It's not right, what will people say? If you let me live, I promise I'll believe in you, I'll worship you, I'll pray every single day, without fail.

Her bare feet enter the old worshipping place, the stones forming their own secret pattern. She puts one foot in front of the other, until she reaches the broken altar, and falls down on hands and knees, pressing one side of her face to the warmth of a stone.

What she hears is the sound of water, running deep, rushing, gushing below, in the core of the earth, this earth. This land.

She looks up at the tall wooden form of the idol, its expression the same, unforgiving, closed to her, and she asks it – do you hear me?

But the idol is not there. It was pulled down long before she was born and strung up as an example in the white man's temple, before being flung onto a ship with all the other gods, and carried away back to those worlds that exist only in her imagination. She closes her eyes, and hears the distant sound of water gurgling.

She sees, herself and Taneipa, at the edge of a river, the Vai'ha, clasping hands, entering inside. They are laughing, trilling with the joy of a new day, of this precious life.

She will wait until the stars come out.

Dear Diary,

I am very sick. Maman will not leave my bedside. I am only able to write just now because she has gone downstairs to receive her students, though I am finding it increasingly difficult to do so, the strength in my arms completely depleted. Maman believes it is because I got soaked in the rain returning home from the ball but the doctor says pneumonia is a viral infection, and one cannot say how it was contracted. Nothing can be done apart from taking rest and drinking plenty of fluids.

My dress is ruined and it is entirely my fault. Silk all the way from China, sighed Maman, and such beautiful handiwork by Fru. Petersen, a small fortune, but never mind that now, you must get better!

Papa wanted to know the day he left, the last time I saw him, what will you say to the boys when they ask who your father is? They never did. I am invisible to them, an ugly duckling beside the tall, beautiful Danes, standing at the edge of the dance floor like an exhibit in The Freak Show.

It had begun to rain when I escaped to the verandah. I should have returned to fetch Maman's stole but I did not want to cross the ballroom again and glimpse their smug faces. I climbed over the balustrade and ran into the darkness, until the music was just a faint hum. When I glanced back, I could see the boys and the girls, like miniature dolls in a playhouse, all lit up. It was at that moment I knew, knew I would never belong in their world, trussed up like a lady. I do not know what my future holds, but I know what I am.

I am my father's daughter, and I would tell the boys, if they cared to ask, my Papa is a painter and a great many men hold him in high regard, the likes of Degas, Monet, and Pisarro to name just a few. And they would say, we have never heard of him, and I would reply, he is in Tahiti painting the savages. Just to see the look in their hateful eyes.

The show was a disaster, as Mormor had predicted. The last letter that Maman received, she refused to share with me, but instead discussed its contents with Mormor, in hushed tones in the dining room. She would only tell me later that none of the paintings sold and he is now planning on returning to Tahiti, so we will not be seeing him again. Am I not allowed to express an opinion on the matter? Did he not ask Maman if we could return with him? Did he not say, give me word, and I will come, arrange everything? Did he not give her his love to give to us, to me?

I have been thinking a great deal during these torturous hours in my bed alone, but then, I am always alone! And I have come to the conclusion that perhaps, they just don't understand – the critics – that perhaps they are scared of his vision, and that he is, truly ahead of his time. Because *Manao Tupapau* spoke to me, speaks to me still, to my soul, though I am loath to admit it. She, the painting, possesses a power beyond this realm, and arouses in one a deep unease, a fear and a wonder, which I can taste, even now, on these parched lips.

In the darkest hour of my sleep, I see her, staring out from her pillow, with secrets inside, behind her brow, upon her tongue. She is privy to a knowledge that will remain hers, and hers alone, while the figure of death crouches at the foot of her bed, his bed, because he has put it there, my Papa.

He is cruel and clever, but she is far cleverer than he, of that I am now certain. Yes, it frightens me, but one day, the world will know it. One day, she will tell her story from beyond the painting.

The daughter leaves the mother's womb from that same mythic opening, the first doorway, out into a room with four solid walls.

She moves across the dance floor, in her gleaming ivory gown, the threads of which were harvested from worms overfed with leaves of the mulberry bush. She does not like the thought of that, still.

She cranes her neck back to gaze at the crystal and gilt chandelier, hanging high above her. The candles have all gone out, the moon, the only source of light. She is reminded of the poem she wrote for her father, never to be shared with him.

My eyes fill with chandelier teardrops,
As I think of you.

A cello begins to rumble out a tune, but there is no band. Everyone has left the ball. She begins to dance regardless, spreading out her thin white arms, which are tender young stems, her hands, buds, which will never bloom. She dances tentatively at first, then with abandon, turning round and around, the silk of her gown burning like a flame in the half-dark. The cello plays on, now the rain, fresh and violent on the rooftops, in the soft grass, on the river, the sea, where it does not make a sound. Soundless night.

The trees once shook, shivered with the moons, and his moans, the moments her father was inside his lover were eternities in her mind.

She continues to dance, moving to the song of the cello, the daughter in death, while her father mourns her, carrying the injustice of god's plan with him to his own grave. She will possess a monument of remembrance carved from dark grey marble. It will be inscribed with her name, and the years that were her short life, and her Papa's tears will be the only flowers she cherishes.

They say I died of Spanish flu.

They say, after you left, I met a young man. He was Tahitian, and we married. We had two children, boys, and these sons of mine were old enough to witness your return. They stood at the doorway of our hut, and watched with bewildered eyes, their mother's exchange with a white stranger.

They do not know what passed between our lips, my sons, but they remember you came back, and asked for me, arriving with legs full of oozing pus-filled sores, and the sight of you made me turn away in disgust. They also say I went back to you, for one, two, three nights, then returned, and climbed, stepped, lay down on the mat beside my gentle, forgiving *tane*. Are there even such men?

They say I died of Spanish flu, in 1918 at the age of 28.

If I were 28, then I would have been one, still sucking my thumb, and clinging to my Foster Mother's skirt when I met you in 1891. Would have been. And yet, yet something does not quite fit, like the dress I wore when I returned to my Foster Mother, stretched tight across my middle, the hem skimming my thighs. The fact is too small for the body of the girl grown.

The certificate of death they find, which a learned man unearths, another white man who wants to write a book about you, your journey, he finds it must be me, because the piece of paper says a girl named Tehaamana died in Mataiea.

So, he writes it down then digs up some details from the mouth of my imaginary son and presents it to the world. I am Tehaamana a Roo who died in 1918 of Spanish flu.

But I never knew her, my namesake, my double. And this white man does not search the gravestones in Mataiea for the girl that is me, I am, have become, I exist, a footnote in your history.

They say I liked earrings, so I must have come from an upper class clan. They say I was of Rarotongan stock, blood, and origin, because I had frizzy hair, which I tamed every morning with coconut oil. They say I was born in Huahine, and brought here as a baby.

Not knowing it would be the beginning of the journey that would take me to you.

Some say I am not real. And I never breathed, lived, or cried. I am bits of your imagination, pieces of all the *vahines* that came to you, and laid down for you, because you were a white man. They even say my name is a trick, a fake, a lie of the light. In truth, I was born Vaiite, which means, the rock pool at the mouth of the river that flows out to the sea, the ocean, and the great beyond. I am proud of that name. My Father gave it to me, half drunk, while my Foster Mother clung to him, then gently pushed him outside.

Another learned man says we were in love because you painted more of me than the others, that your pictures of me were your best, most terrifying and beautiful, beautiful and terrifying, and yes, at the time, I was scared, but not of the dead, as you said, as you said, as it is written.

It was clear we were in love. Were we...in love? You were a man, sick with life, while I was a girl, just beginning, blooming, when you took me, suddenly, plucked my young stem with your stained hands, with fingernails dug deep with colour. And I went with you, like a hog to the slaughter.

Some say they don't want to know my story, our story, because of you, of what you represent and they hate you for it, with all their heart, what you did. How dare you? They say you were like the rest of them, the colonisers, and they have a point. It must be said. And yet, they cannot say why, why I am on their rum bottles, and biscuit tins, packets of tea, English Breakfast and Earl Grey, in every Carrefour, and gift shop, a reproduction of the girl in the blue and white striped dress that does not belong to her.

They say it was the times. It was what they all did back then, the men, far from home, the white ones like you. But. They fucked little girls in your world too, between the dark streets, and the soiled sheets in the houses of your cities. The ones who don't want to know prefer I am fourteen, even better if I am fifteen. I must be, because that is the body of a woman lying naked across your bed. You write I am thirteen, and you call me Tehura, because you take a liking to the name.

The ones who think they know, say I was younger, eleven in truth.

And the ones who truly know say they don't know anything about me. They say they cannot tell. Cannot speak what happened, because they are duty-bound to keep it from the white man, from intruders, from those who don't belong to the land.

And they do not care what is written, was written, or will be, because I am theirs, and I am buried here, in their soil, in this little village of Faaone, where I was born, and raised, and where you came when I was old enough, when I was still young, where you took me, then raped me. But that was after.

They say they brought me back, to clean me, and care for me, to make me comfortable after you had broken, all of me.

I am here. Here I am.

I am everywhere. Not in the ground where my bones lie, where I am buried in the position I assumed in my first mother's belly, that's how they hid me, as I grew the first nine months of my life, my forehead pressed to my knees.

They pushed into my fist, a page of The Good Book, the very first page, that told how your God made the world in seven days – six, because on the seventh He took rest. They buried me like this.

This is your resting place, they said, and we will always keep it, keep you. Keep your secret.

They say I did not die of syphilis, the sickness, which the English called The Spanish Disease, and the Spanish called The French Disease. Then the French came. And you, your men christened it The British Disease. No, I did not die of it, because all the others lived to tell the tale, the women who birthed at least one child of yours.

Just a simple stone, a small boulder marks my resting place, with no marks on it, so no one would know, so the white man would never come looking. Now worms and insects crawl through the earth that fills my skull and they make their home there, where there are no more thoughts.

None.

Here I am.

I am here.

Everywhere. In the nut of the *mape* which spells death, in the kiss of the sun which grants life, in the smile of the eel which reveals its face then disappears into the depths of the water, in the sacred stones of the *marae* that have been carried out from the mountain and laid down in a new place for the people to come and see and wonder. And remember.

I am in the wooden carvings of our ancient gods trapped behind glass, now called Art Exhibits of the Archipelagos. I am in the faces of the men, the children, and the women, in their wide, beautiful faces, in the crowds of people in this landing place, who wait, their hope overshadowed by the mountains beyond. I am in the women who dance on a raised stage with practiced ease, who greet the visitors, the strangers that still come, while their men accompany them on ukuleles, joyous, yet defeated. I am in the song of the cockerel. Cockadoodledoo!

I am in the call of the scavenging ground dove that parades through the din of the life that presses on all sides. Kikoo! Kikoo!

I am in the heady scent of the gardenia, the wild jasmine, and the five-fingered *tiare* Apetahi that grows only on the slopes of Mount Temehani. I am in the wrinkled, hardened hands of the mother and the father, in the dreams of the son and the daughter-in-law, in the confused eyes of the grandchild. I am in them all, they who express their love, their grief, in this leaving place, by bringing garlands of shells to hang around one another's necks. I am in their tears.

I am in the fearlessness of the young who have reclaimed the past and wear their ancestor's names inscribed on their skin with pride. I am in the compass of the stars, Inseparable and her twin-brother, who shine hard and bright and close, so very close, without fail each night.

I am in Tahiti, inside it, bound, and yet I am free.

I am in the whisper of the wind through the leaves, which tremble in the branches of the trees, like the pages of your book, like the river in spate, like raindrops on a roof of *pandanu* leaf, like the ocean, always, at the edges of everything.

I am in the stork, in its brilliant white wings, flying high, etched against the deep, the blue. The sky.

I am in the dark light of the moon, suspended in one half of a shell, which belonged to Ta'aroa.

And beyond the lagoon, the waves still crash.

I can smell the earth, the world waking up.

This is my body, my voice.

Acknowledgements

The myths and legends that inspired my own retelling of them can be found in the following texts: Hieronymus Fracastor's Syphilis, from the original Latin; a translation in prose of the immortal poem by Giralomo Fracastoro (The Philmar Company, St. Louis, MO, 1911); Noa Noa by Paul Gauguin, translated from French by O.F. Theis (N. L. Brown, New York, 1919); Ancient Tahiti by Teuira Henry (Bernice P. Bishop Museum, Bulletin n. 48, Honolulu, 1928); Legends of the South Seas by Anthony Alpers (John Murray, 1970); Ancient Tahitian Society by Douglas L. Oliver (The University Press of Hawaii, Honolulu, 1974); and Legends of the Archipelagos, Volume 1, by Natea Montelier Tetanui (Department of Culture and Heritage of French Polynesia, 2016). The song of Ta'aroa is taken in its near original rendition from Gauguin's Noa Noa. Some phrases from Tii's procreation story are also borrowed from Gauguin's Noa Noa.

I am deeply indebted to the following people who assisted my research in Tahiti: Miriama Bono, Henri Brillant, Poerani Ebb, Brenda Chin Foo, Daniel Magueron, Roti Make, Allegra Marshall, Riccardo Pineri, Lena Ram, Bruno Saura, Isabelle Tai, Leonard Tauapaohu, Josiane Teamotuaitau, Maruake Tehiva, Lanihei Tehiva, and Natea Montelier Tetanui. Special thanks to: Jurate Aglinskaite, Waleed Akhtar, Dhana Luxmi Balasubramanian, Alan Bett, Sonia Castang, Amy Gwatkin, Jay Kirkland, Rose McDonagh, Pamela Moffat, Emma Claire Sweeney, Creative Scotland, and The Saltire Society. Sincere and grateful thanks to three important people, for their passion to get this story out into the world: my agent, Jonathan Ruppin; my editor, Leonora Rustamova; and my publisher, Kevin Duffy. Very special thanks to my mother, Sarojana Ponnambalam, for all her love and support over the years, and to Graham Clark, my *tane*, my love, my rock in the ocean.

About the Author

Devika Ponnambalam was born in 1969 in Bandar Seri Begawan, Brunei, came to the UK at the age of eight, and grew up in London. She graduated from the National Film and Television School in Fiction Directing in 1998, with an award-winning short film, and has received film commissions from the Arts Council of England, Film Four and the British Film Institute. She has also directed for mainstream TV in the UK, and in Malaysia. In 2004, Devika graduated with an MA in Creative Writing (Prose) from the University of East Anglia, where she began writing this book. In 2018, she travelled to Tahiti with the assistance of a research and development grant awarded by Creative Scotland. She lives in Roslin, Midlothian.